Once more, he pressed the pen to the paper.

My dear Miss Younger, he wrote.

But she was not his dear. They had never met. He wadded the paper and shoved it to a corner of the large, polished desk.

"My dear Miss Dollar Princess," he mumbled.

Miss Younger, he scratched across the fresh page. *I hope this letter finds you well.*

That was easily written, since it was true. Now, what to say?

I look forward to traveling to New York and to meeting you, at last.

This was not as true as hoping she was well was.

"I look forward to meeting you in New York, where I will gain your fortune and you will gain my title," he mumbled.

The truth was, he dreaded meeting this stranger he was contracted to wed. He'd known title seekers all his life.

Hopefully Miss Lilleth Younger was a decent woman. And yet the question remained, why would she be willing to sell herself for social status…? One did have to wonder.

Curse it, though, he was no better than she was, selling himself for her fortune.

Author Note

Many thanks for your interest in the story of Lilleth Younger and River Halston as they enter a marriage of convenience.

Marriages of this sort can be tricky things given that they are typically committed in order to avoid something even trickier.

In some cases, the reason is to escape an unsavory suitor. In others, it is to ensure the financial solvency of one's title.

Lilleth and River wed for both of those reasons.

For many couples, marriage will be disappointing. But for others, the lucky ones, marriage will be joyful and loving.

Which, do you suppose, will it be for our newlyweds?

Given that Lilleth and River live within the pages of a romance novel, you can guess that they will be among the joyful and loving.

How ever will they get there, though? Our Lilleth envisions joyful times and many babies, while our River is set on having a sterile marriage with no more passion than it takes to beget the required heir.

Naturally, here in our world of happily-ever-after, love does find a way.

THE VISCOUNT'S DOLLAR PRINCESS

CAROL ARENS

Recycling programs for this product may not exist in your area.

ISBN-13: 978-1-335-05032-8

The Viscount's Dollar Princess

For questions and comments about the quality of this book, please contact us at CustomerService@Harlequin.com.

Harlequin Enterprises ULC
22 Adelaide St. West, 41st Floor
Toronto, Ontario M5H 4E3, Canada
www.Harlequin.com

HarperCollins Publishers
Macken House, 39/40 Mayor Street Upper,
Dublin 1, D01 C9W8, Ireland
www.HarperCollins.com

Printed in U.S.A.

1 2 3 4 5 6 7 8 9 10 HDC 28 27 26 25

Carol Arens delights in tossing fictional characters into hot water, watching them steam and then giving them a happily-ever-after. When she is not writing, she enjoys spending time with her family, beach camping or lounging about a mountain cabin. At home, she enjoys playing with her grandchildren and gardening. During rare spare moments, you will find her snuggled up with a good book. Carol enjoys hearing from readers at carolarens@yahoo.com or on Facebook.

Books by Carol Arens

Harlequin Historical

The Cowboy's Convenient Wife
The Truth Behind the Governess
Marriage Charade with the Heir
The Gentleman's Cinderella Bride
Meeting Her Promised Viscount
The Viscount's Christmas Proposal
"A Kiss Under the Mistletoe"
in *A Victorian Family Christmas*
To Wed a Wallflower
The Viscount's Yuletide Bride

The Rivenhall Weddings

Inherited as the Gentleman's Bride
In Search of a Viscountess
A Family for the Reclusive Baron

Visit the Author Profile page
at Harlequin.com for more titles.

This book is for my daughter, Linda Lopez. Cheers to long shopping trips to the nursery in search of the perfect plant and fueled by the perfect latte.

Chapter One

June 5, 1884, 11:47p.m., London

River Halston, Viscount Aberly, picked up his pen, stared at the inky tip and then set it down in favor of listening to rain tap the library window behind him.

Perhaps if he wrote the letter, signed it and prepared it for the post, he would sleep the night through without the nightmare that had been plaguing him. He might no longer have hellish visions of his small nieces and his widowed sister-in-law wearing cast-off clothing and living in a run-down flat, their elegant home sold to a stranger…or worse, to someone they knew.

Logically, he would never allow that to happen. Logic, however had nothing to do with fears that plagued a man in the wee hours. Anxiety over bankruptcy claimed him nearly every night of late.

Pushing back from his desk, he rose then strode to the fireplace where he stood with his hands clasped behind his back, as deep in thought as he'd ever been.

Perhaps a way to begin the letter would come to him while staring at the flames.

He would ask his sister-in-law for advice, but she and his young nieces were abed hours ago.

Not that Clara would have advice to help. His situation remained as it was.

Loving one woman, he would marry another.

For the sake of the Aberly Estate and for all the souls in his care he'd put aside his beloved fiancée, Alicia, and would now wed a wealthy stranger.

River alone would pay the price for the financial ruin his father had heaped upon Aberly at his death. How long had it been since the man even glanced at the accounts he was responsible for?

Circling the room, River came back to the desk.

Normally he was a decisive man, competent in every situation…not this one, though.

The fact that the woman he had intended to marry was not grieving the loss of their future as he was doing ought to rally his pride, stiffen his upper lip. It ought to be easier moving on with his life.

The anguish of it was that Alicia had wed a dashing young fellow of lesser title but great fortune within three months of River being forced to call off their engagement.

What misery he endured whenever he crossed paths with her. Alicia was abloom in happiness.

It had been a jolt to his soul discovering that she had not felt the blow fate dealt them the way he did.

Sitting down with a decisive thump, River pressed on with the letter. The sooner he finished the task, the sooner he would be in bed gathering strength for the challenges of the next day.

A man did not live up to his title by remaining awake into the late hours. It was an irresponsible use of time and energy.

Indeed, had the fourth Viscount not spent the wee hours

of the night in wasteful living, the fifth Viscount would not be facing financial ruin.

One thing River would never be was a man like his father.

He would pay the ransom required of him and wed the American dollar princess looming in his future.

And perhaps have a night's sleep without seeing small Victoria wearing a ragged dress and having no proper doll to play with.

Once more, he pressed the pen to the paper.

My Dear Miss Younger, he wrote.

But she was not his dear, they had never met. He wadded the paper and shoved it to a corner of the large polished desk.

"My dear Miss Dollar Princess," he mumbled.

Miss Younger, he scratched across the fresh page. *I hope this letter finds you well.*

That was easily written since it was true. It did not bear thinking what would happen to them all if she fell victim to ill health or anything else.

Now what to say?

I look forward to traveling to New York and to meeting you, at last.

This was not as true as hoping she was well was.

"I look forward to meeting you in New York where I will gain your fortune and you will gain my title," he mumbled.

The truth was, he dreaded meeting this stranger he was contracted to wed. He'd known title seekers all his life. After his mother's death, his father had dallied with several of them.

Hopefully, Miss Lilleth Younger was a decent woman. And yet the question remained, why would she be willing to sell herself for social status…? One did have to wonder.

Curse it, though, he was no better than she was, selling himself for her fortune.

I trust that the arrangements made for the wedding ceremony by your mother and Miss Deborah Newton are satisfactory.

What were the arrangements, he wondered. His part was to arrive in New York City a week before his nuptials. He was to recite his vows, receive a wife and a fortune, which would secure the future of his family, his title, and all who depended upon it for their livelihood.

Details of pomp and circumstance were better left to his late brother's wife, Clara, and Clara's aunt, Miss Deborah Newton.

It was not as if each flower bud or romantic piece of music represented heartfelt vows of love and devotion.

Given how easily Alicia had set him aside, he wondered if love and devotion in marriage was simply a fool's fantasy.

I wish to assure you that I will work diligently to protect and increase all that you entrust to me financially. I do not take this responsibility lightly.

This line was earnestly written. One thing he would not be was a reckless guardian of the fortune she was committing to him.

As far as how they would get on as Viscount and Viscountess…husband and wife, he could not say.

One thing was certain, he would not trustingly hand over his affections to the woman as he had to Alicia.

I realize a lady of your position might have her pick of eligible gentlemen, and so I am appreciative of—

That was better left unsaid since he understood that she could not have her pick of men and it was why she had chosen him.

He tossed the letter and wrote it over again, leaving off the part about her pick of gentlemen.

Rest assured I offer you the protection of my home and my name.

In spite of the fact that they were strangers, she would soon be his wife and therefore he would act as her champion in whichever situation she required him to be.

With no idea of what else to write, he ended with, *I pray that you have a safe and comfortable journey to New York where I anticipate meeting you.*

He actually did pray for her safety since he understood the lady to be at some risk in Connecticut.

Admittedly, the prayer was for his family as well as Miss Younger because without her Aberly would fail.

Regards, River Halston, Viscount Aberly.

That last would not do. Those words were too formal for a lady one was to wed, even though he had never communicated with her before.

It was a lucky thing he had a large stack of stationary, for he crushed yet another letter and tossed it away.

Beginning again, he carefully considered each word. This time he ended it, *With my best regards, River Halston.*

With that awkward chore finished, he put the letter in an envelope for his secretary to post tomorrow.

Still, he remained at his desk listening to rain pinging on the window glass.

The letter had been all about duty and his promise to live up to it. But now his thoughts went another direction. What was she like, this woman he would share a future with?

Was she pretty? Not that it mattered, but he was a man and so the thought did present.

Alicia had been known for her beauty, a lady of elegance and refined manners that she had learned from birth.

But what of the woman he would wed?

Was she cheerful or serious minded?

Serious minded he hoped. The last sort of woman he wanted was one who would tempt him to cast off accountability in favor of jolly amusement.

What his father left behind after his death had taught a hard lesson.

July 4, 1884, 10:00 p.m,. Apple Valley Acres, Devotion Springs, Connecticut

From where Lilleth Younger stood beside the window in the darkened study she watched a hundred or more people outside gazing up in wonder at fireworks blooming in the sky. What a sight it was, so many colors reflecting in the lake and drizzling down.

Papa would have loved it. She had the most comforting sensation that his spirit was standing beside her, smiling the same as she was.

Folks had traveled from neighboring towns to watch the firework show that Apple Valley Acres put on every year. Papa had begun the tradition before Lilleth was born. Although he had been gone for more than two years now, she and Mama carried on with the celebration.

Guests, as well as farmhands and their families, had arrived early this morning. This afternoon there had been a barbecue and dancing. The farm was well-known for the celebration in honor of the nation's founding. Even the governor and his family attended most years.

For a man who had grown up on a humble ranch in Texas, Papa did enjoy putting on a lavish party.

As much as Lilleth longed to be outside with the guests, circumstance kept her standing in the dark room.

Those troublesome Snell men were out there, lurking about like bobcats sniffing prey…her being the prey. As neighbors went, Slade and his sons were as bad as they came.

Even before Papa went to his Maker that blackhearted family had lusted after Apple Valley Acres and the fine, expensive horses bred here.

But they could not get this prime land without one of them wedding her.

Given the chance, those greedy souls would ruin Apple Valley Acres as thoroughly as they had their own ranch. She did not mean Homer, though. He was not like the rest of his family. The youngest Snell was a decent boy and her friend. He must have taken after his mama, she thought, but could not say for certain since the poor woman hadn't lasted four years into her forced marriage.

Apparently the Snells did not know how to get a bride except to kidnap her. Certainly no reasonable woman would agree to join that family of gamblers who reveled in wasteful living.

"And you think you'll get my property? Everything Papa worked so hard for?" she muttered while watching colorful lights exploding over the water. "You will not have it or me."

And the reason they would not had to do with the letter growing damp from her gripping it so hard.

She turned up the lamp furthest from the window.

It wasn't like her to be nervous, but this letter was her first communication from the stranger she was going to marry. That sort of thing didn't happen to a girl every day.

In the normal way of things young people fell in love, and then after a romantic courtship, got married. It would not be so for Lilleth. Lilleth's hopeful suitors were threatened with bodily harm.

More than that, though, she had made her father a promise.

Because of it she'd had no opportunity to fall in love.

Which might be just as well since she had no wish to leave behind a lover when she fulfilled Papa's last wish for her.

That wish being for her to wed a British nobleman! Papa had taken Mama from Society when they wed and wished for her to have it back…to have his family gain higher social status than he'd been able to provide.

Papa died before said nobleman could be found but to Mama's delight, her English cousin, Deborah Newton, knew of a gentleman who would suit.

Of course Lilleth had agreed to marry the man. There was nothing she would not do to please her father, even if his view of events was now as far away as Heaven.

She clutched the letter from the Viscount, who Father's wealth had purchased, so tightly that it might be too wrinkled to read.

Unfolding the paper, she wondered what her future husband would have to say in their first correspondence.

It would be reasonable for him to tell her a bit about himself, what he liked and didn't like. What made him happy and what made him sad. Just a bit about himself so they wouldn't meet as strangers.

How, she quite naturally wondered, did the Viscount feel about marrying her? Did he wonder what she felt about marrying him?

She smoothed the paper and held it close to the light, squinting a bit because she'd turned the lamp so dim.

Miss Younger,

She read through it quickly, scanning over how he hoped she was well…that he looked forward to meeting…and so on.

His mention of the wedding was as brief as could be. No sense of eager anticipation whatsoever.

"My mother and her cousin went to every effort to make our wedding more than satisfactory." Indeed, the event was bound to be quite beautiful. "I do wish you had more to say about it…but I do like what you have to say about increasing my money."

When she read down to the words where he offered the protection of his name and his home, she sighed hard. That could not come soon enough.

Only days ago Coulder, the eldest Snell son, might have succeeded in ambushing her had Homer not sabotaged the attempt by charging his horse at his brother's hiding place while singing a bawdy song at the top of his lungs and alerting her to the danger.

What a bit of good fortune that she had been riding Arrow, the fastest horse in the stable. Unless she missed her guess, with all the distraction Homer caused, Coulder did not realize how close he had come to capturing her.

Shaking off a chill at the near calamity, she read on about River Halston's wish for her safe journey to New York.

As a note of becoming acquainted went, it wasn't much. Lilleth turned the paper over hoping he'd gone into more detail on the back side of the page.

"Dull as bones," she muttered. "I hope you are a bit cheerier than this letter indicates."

As it stood, she didn't know the man she was to marry any better than if he had not written. For all that both Mama and cousin Deborah remembered River Halston to be a happy, smiling baby, it did not come across in his letter.

"I will communicate better in my response," she said to the elegant scrawl of his pen across the fancy paper with his title embossed on it.

Bending low, she dashed past the window and went to the desk, all the while listening for footsteps on the rug in the corridor.

More and more, outwitting her foes was a challenge. The closer her wedding to the Viscount came, the more hell-bent they were on having her first.

She would not fret about them now. She had an important letter to write.

Lilleth lit the desk lamp, turning the flame only bright enough to write by. From her desk drawer, she withdrew several sheets of paper with the Apple Valley Acres brand printed…not embossed, on the top. She took out the ink and unstoppered the bottle.

Dear River,
Howdy, I was pleased to receive your letter.

Perhaps she ought to use a different greeting than *howdy.* It was not the most elegant word but it was the one her father had always used.

Even after he moved to New York in order to sell iron to railroad men, her father's Texas upbringing echoed in his speech.

Not that the way he spoke prevented him from earning a fortune. Papa's business sense had left her as rich as a queen.

Lilleth was the product of two worlds, Papa's cowboy past and Mama's genteel English upbringing.

Both had gone into making her who she was… Lilleth Younger of Apple Valley Acres. Soon Father would have his wish and she would live both sides of her heritage.

"I'd have been better pleased if you told me something about yourself," she muttered to an invisible fiancé.

She gripped the pen between her fingers and wrote, *I, too, look forward to meeting you in New York. And to seeing what color your hair is and the shade of your eyes. Had you enclosed a photograph of yourself, I could picture what our future children might look like.*

Oh, but what did it matter, really? She would wed him regardless of his looks. It was not as if there was someone else brave enough to ask for her hand. Men had a tendency to value the body parts that the Snells threatened to cut from them.

I do hope you enjoy singing, she continued. *For I do it often. Would you say you are accomplished at kissing women? For I have never been kissed but am eager to know about it.*

Mama always did say Lilleth was far too curious.

I do hope you laugh easily and take pleasure in little things. I cannot imagine life with a sour Sam... and I fear that your letter indicates you might be. Where, I ask is the smile my mother and Deborah Newton remember?

No place was where.

Lilleth ripped the letter in quarters then quarters again.

On a fresh sheet she wrote,

Mr. Halston... Wait…that was wrong.

On another sheet, she wrote,

Lord Aberly,
I was quite pleased to receive your letter and I hope that mine, in return, finds you well. I, too, look forward to making your acquaintance in New York. I am confident that my mother and Miss Deborah Newton have planned a wedding that you will approve of.

Nothing made Mama happier than planning Lilleth's wedding had. She claimed it made her feel like a girl again from back in the days when she was a baron's daughter.

Mama hadn't smiled much since Papa died. She had loved Papa with all her heart.

Even though her mother had never uttered a word of regret for leaving England, Lilleth wondered if there was a beat or two of her heart that she had left behind when she went off and married a poor American who had yet to make his fortune.

More than once over the years, Lilleth had caught her mother looking east as if she could see across the Atlantic Ocean, all the way to England.

I do appreciate that you will be a responsible steward of the inheritance my father left me, she wrote.

She appreciated it more than he could know…the Snells would run through it in a year if they got their hands on it.

The promise of the protection of River Halston's home and his name could not be more important to her or to Mama…or to everyone who called Apple Valley Acres home.

Because of everything the Viscount offered to her and Mama, she did not regret making an arranged marriage. Many young ladies of great wealth did the same, even in America.

Besides, something had happened to Mama on the day

that Lilleth agreed to the marriage. It was as if she'd come back to life after Papa's death.

While Mama did not wish to live anyplace but her beloved horse ranch, where she had lived since well before Lilleth was born, she did claim that she would be thrilled to step back into Society for short periods of time.

I also pray that you have a safe and comfortable voyage to New York.

All best wishes until we meet in the autumn,

Miss Lilleth Younger

It was growing quiet outside. Soon people would be coming in and settling into their rooms for the night. The house was huge and guests often remained until morning. Farmhands would bed down in the bunkhouse while the married hands would retire to their cabins with their wives and children.

Folding the letter, she put it in an envelope for the farm's bookkeeper to take to Devotion Springs with the rest of the outgoing mail.

Then she simply sat where she was, feeling the house wrap her up in peace.

She loved her home, every green hill and valley, each fresh stream that watered the land, was as dear as her next breath.

New York was bound to seem as foreign a place as the moon.

Lilleth was as far from being a city girl as could be. In fact, she had never been to a large city, preferring to be in the company of her horses...riding them over lush green acres.

It was going to take a mighty metamorphosis to turn this rural girl into Viscountess Aberly.

Life was going to change and there was no choice but to change along with it.

Out in the hallway she heard Mama speaking with John Dalton, the farm manager, thanking him for all he did to make the night a success.

John was more like an uncle to her than a hired manager. She would not think about how much she would miss him and everyone else who made this farm a success, not right now. There would be time for that later.

Now though, she dabbed at a tear because this was probably her last Independence Day party and she'd been forced to watch it from inside.

New York was bound to be dull as bones compared to fireworks blooming over the lake.

But no, she would not cry.

She would sing…rejoice that a way had presented which would keep everyone living here secure and would allow the horse ranch to go on as it always had…except without her.

Chapter Two

As much as Lilleth wished to step into her new role as Viscountess with a positive attitude and view life as a song with a new verse added, saying goodbye to the old was heart-wrenching.

Having just dropped off gifts for each of the twenty orphans at Mary Clinger's Home for Children in Devotion Springs, Lilleth stood on the porch for a moment tugging her coat against the cold wind and listening to the little ones laughing inside.

With fall settling in the weather was turning. Even with her thick collar turned up, nippy air chilled her neck.

Going down the steps Lilleth thought about how the children here counted upon the support of Apple Valley Acres.

There were some matters which would need to be worked out between her and the man she was going to marry when it came to her money.

She mounted her horse, settled in for the long ride back to the farm. Giving a backward glance, she thought of how she would miss coming here.

"I suppose everything I've got, including you, is going to belong to Viscount Aberly soon." She reached down to pat Arrow's glistening brown neck. The swift, powerful animal was the only one she rode these days when she was out of sight of the house. He could outrun any horse the Snells owned. "But don't you worry I intend to have a say in how he spends my money. Mary Clinger will get her monthly allowance just like always and you will still get your apples."

Riding warmed her somewhat. With leaves turning shades of gold and red, the scenery was spectacular. The journey between Devotion Springs and the entrance gate of Apple Valley Acres passed as easily as a sigh.

Not a ripple of trouble anywhere and she had been alert for it. With such a short time remaining until she went to New York, extra caution was called for.

She'd just ridden under the carved wooden sign indicating she was on Apple Valley Acres and within sight of the white mansion she'd called home for all her life, when she decided to visit the family cemetery. It was not quite a mile west of the long driveway leading to the house so she turned her horse in that direction.

The next week would be busy so she would take this time to say goodbye to the loved ones buried here.

A grove of trees shaded the area, their yellow leaves twisting in a cool breeze. Under the trees was a white picket fence marking the area where some of her family rested in peace.

Lilleth had grown up as an only child, although she'd had two older brothers. A pair of small marble crosses stood guard over them.

"I'm sorry I never knew you Eric and Benny," she said still sitting in Arrow's saddle.

Her brothers had been born in New York while Papa was earning his fortune, but they had succumbed to measles within a week of one another.

Mama had been so heartsick that Papa despaired of losing her, too.

It was why he'd sold the New York mansion and taken Mama to live permanently at their horse ranch in Connecticut.

Mama's love of horses was what finally brought her back to herself…that and having Lilleth.

As far as Lilleth knew, Mama had never gone back to the city, not even to visit, even though Papa often traveled there for business.

Lilleth had never been allowed to go with him. Mama feared the same disease which took her sons would find her daughter.

Since Mama's feelings were more important to Lilleth than visiting New York was, she had never pressed the issue. Besides, like Mama, she was happiest here, free to roam these vast green acres.

One day Lilleth would have a large family. Her children would have many brothers and sisters. If it was within her power, they would never seek the company of gravestones.

She shifted her gaze from Benny's small cross to Papa's big one.

"I'm going away soon, Papa. Life is calling me away, just like you said it would."

She supposed she was not really saying goodbye since Papa and her brothers lived in her heart, not the ground.

Still, it seemed fitting to say some words…or better, sing them a song.

A breeze came up, whispering through tall grass as if in accompaniment to her voice.

She sang "Shenandoah" because it was a song of longing and there was one verse that seemed especially fitting.

"'I'm being bound away…'" The words carried across the land in the cold wind.

She would have probably wept by the time she came to the end of the song, but she spotted a rider coming over the rise of the hill and the song died on her lips.

It could be anyone. But it also could be a Snell. She rose in the stirrups, drew her rifle out of the saddle holster while looking hard across the open meadow.

Although she'd been raised a lady, Papa had insisted she learn to use a weapon in case she needed to defend herself or the horses against a bear or a bobcat.

So far, she had not faced such a danger. This was Connecticut not Texas, after all.

Closer now, she saw that the rider was slight of build. He waved his arm, his hat gripped in his fist. A flash of red hair glinted in the late afternoon sunshine.

She sat down with a thump which gave Arrow a start.

"It's only Homer," she explained, sliding her weapon back into the sheath. "But he sure is in a hurry."

"Lills!" he shouted then bent low over his mount's neck urging the horse faster.

She raced Arrow toward him.

When Homer reached her, he was as winded as his horse was. "Lucky thing I found you."

"What's wrong?" she asked because something sure was.

"You've got to go, Lills," he panted.

Homer was the only one who called her "Lills." It gave her heart a squeeze thinking of how she much she would miss his wide toothy grin and the shock of red hair which he could never tame.

"Pa's getting itchy about that fella from England. He means to hitch you up with Coulder and you know he's the worst one of us all. I tried to get Pa to pick me for you but he called me a runt who wouldn't have children. I wish he'd picked me. I wouldn't treat you mean."

"I know you wouldn't. You've always been a dear friend. Mama and I will be leaving quite soon. I sure will miss you."

He did not flash his endearing grin. His red brows furrowed.

"But they're coming for you tonight. Pa already kidnapped Reverend Willis and has him tied to a chair in the kitchen. You've got to go now."

Homer drew his mount close beside Arrow. He leaned sideways and kissed her cheek. "I wouldn't have been a bad husband to you, Lills. I'll ride back to the house with you, make sure you get there safe."

She blinked away moisture while listening to Homer's horse galloping behind her.

Homer was only nineteen and too young to wed, but not too young to have a noble heart.

From the time Lilleth rushed inside the house and informed her mother of what was about to happen and the time Lilleth was riding away from home with the sun going down behind her had been no more than thirty minutes.

Mama had appeared collected at the news, but that was her way. While Lilleth changed into the pants which Mama insisted she wear, her mother had ordered Arrow to remain saddled and food packed for her journey.

A journey which could not be traveled by train, according to Mama. In a very short time the Snells would discover her absence and the station would be the first place they would search.

Mama's rushed orders while hugging Lilleth goodbye were to stay near small towns but not to enter them unless there was an emergency. Once she got to New York, she was to go first thing to Sutter Hotel near Central Park where the rooms were reserved in advance. The accountant had already opened a bank account for them at J.P. Morgan if she needed extra funds.

Also, once she arrived Lilleth was to wear the serviceable dress packed in her saddlebag. The less attention she attracted the safer she would be.

Although it must be cutting Mama to her soul to be sending Lilleth away alone and unprotected, it was the way it must be. Anyone watching the house would become suspicious if she and Mama both went madly dashing away from Apple Valley Acres at this time of evening.

Better for her to go alone, give the impression of being a stable hand casually riding to town. John wanted to come with her but Mama pointed out that he was needed to help direct the Snells away from Lilleth.

The last thing her mother told her was that her viscount should have already arrived at Sutter Hotel. If there was trouble, she could turn to him.

So, off she'd gone. In the closing of the door, she'd heard Mama call, "John! Load the weapons!"

By the time Lilleth reached the wooden arch which marked the farm's property line, darkness had fully settled.

Being out at night did not trouble her. Many were the times she and Papa had spent the night outdoors, especially when the mares were getting near foaling time.

Crickets and owls were a lullaby to her. Not that she would sing along tonight as she sometimes did. Silence was the order of business tonight.

The journey would only take her about a day and a half riding Arrow.

“Good boy, Arrow, good boy,” she murmured, reaching down to pat his neck.

Urgency being the matter of the moment, she did not think to be sad at leaving, only that poor Reverend Willis must be frantic.

Chapter Three

After a day and a half of travel with no trouble whatsoever, Lilleth was in New York, riding Arrow down 5th Avenue, her eyes too wide to blink.

She led the horse though canyons made of buildings instead of hillsides. She had an ache in her neck from gazing up at what seemed to be miles of windows and rooftops. Everywhere she looked there was something new and exciting to see.

Given that her travels previously hadn't taken her much farther than Devotion Springs, she had never seen anything as remarkable as this city. How did builders stack structures so high without them toppling over?

No one seemed worried at the prospect. Passing by in fancy open-air buggies people laughed and chattered. Ladies dressed as if they were on their way to a fairy tale. She had never dreamed so much lace existed in the world.

Or so much noise. She had a time of it, maneuvering Arrow in and out of traffic. The poor fellow was nervous with all the hustle and bustle going on around him.

Luckily, the Sutter Hotel soon came into sight. The first thing she did was settle Arrow into the hotel's stable. Next, she changed into the workday dress Mama had packed in her saddlebag.

But what to do with her weapon? Since she did not see anyone else carrying weapons, she decided it would be best to leave it locked in her hotel room.

Perhaps New York was a safe city.

At last, she was ready to get herself settled. A bath sounded just the thing.

She walked through some pretty gardens on the way from the stable to the rear of the hotel building thinking of how nice a bath would be. A brick path led her around the side and then to the front of Sutter Hotel.

Once standing before the entry doors, she found it difficult to get her feet to move toward them.

She was too awestruck to do anything but stare.

Was there anything as elegant as the pair of huge glass doors in shiny brass frames?

There was even a man dressed in a black suit and white shirt whose sole job seemed to be opening those fancy doors for guests.

While she tried to get her feet to step forward, she watched two women, one with what had to be a dozen feathers on her hat and the other with some small white-furred dead creature circling her throat, it's dried out little paws crossed to keep it fastened about the wearer's neck.

The ladies showed no hesitation in walking toward the door with barely a nod at the man.

It might not be charitable to think so, but a thought was a thought whether one wished it to be or not…so, it looked to Lilleth as if a giant penguin was greeting a pair of peacocks.

After the women went inside, he opened the door for a pair of gentlemen wearing tall black hats.

As far as she knew Papa had never worn one like that, the Texan in him preferring his Stetson.

What kind of fancy place must this be to have a someone whose job it was to open the door for perfectly able people?

Settling her saddlebag over her shoulder she walked toward the man attending the door…who looked a hundred times more elegant than she did.

He made no move to allow her to enter, but simply stared down his nose at her.

Perhaps it was her rifle making his round eyes grow even rounder. She had to carry it in view, though, since it was too long to put in her saddle pack.

"Howdy," she said offering the friendly smile that he withheld from her.

"The servant's entrance is in the rear of the hotel."

"Why, thank you, sir, but I don't require a servant. If you will direct me to my suite of rooms, I'd be grateful."

The fellow looked down his nose at her more arrogantly than before. He hadn't done so to those other women he'd opened the door for.

Maybe she ought to follow her mother's advice and call on the Viscount for help.

But no, she would figure a way in on her own. If she could not, she'd sleep in the stable next to Arrow.

She gave the look back to the man, but had to look up her nose at him, not down.

"Step aside, sir, I will open the door myself."

She gave him the imperious glance that Mama used when she wanted to get her way. It was a skill Mama had gained from growing up a baron's daughter.

With an ungentlemanly grunt, the man opened the door.

What did it matter that he didn't smile at her like he had the others? She was inside and that was what mattered.

Being weary from travel she could nearly hear that bath calling her name and afterward, a nap.

The first thing she noticed crossing the room was that there was music. The hotel in Devotion Springs did not have music.

Glancing about she saw four musicians on a raised platform and behind them a stained glass window which must have been twenty feet tall. They were playing one of her favorite pieces of music. She had half a mind to hum along but people were already sliding her curious looks.

And no wonder they were. She'd be staring at herself if she were them.

She must look like a pebble tossed into a handful of diamonds. While the other ladies wore silky-looking footwear, she still had on her worn and dusty riding boots. Compared to their satin and lace, her cotton dress was drab…dowdy even.

And the rifle set her apart, a clear reminder that she was no longer in Devotion Springs.

Very well, let folks stare at her. She didn't mind so much. Probably because she was staring too, and in more astonishment than they were.

She took slow steps toward the front desk because there was just so much glamour a person could take in all at once…and what was that?

Just there in the center of the big lobby was one of the most amazing things she had ever seen. A giant swan formed of ice, its wings stretched as if it would fly up to the ceiling. Just wait until Mama got a look at it.

Lilleth changed direction and walked toward the sculpture. She paused for a moment to take in the wonder of such a thing.

The peacock ladies were also standing beside the ice bird, admiring the glistening spectacle.

"It's something special they brought in for the Viscount,"

the one with the feathers on her hat commented to her companion.

Why, she'd known her fiancé was a man of importance but to have an ice sculpture set up in his honor was quite something.

"There are more flowers in the lobby than usual, too. Lord Aberly is to be wed, you know. It is why he has come from England…but perhaps one of us will snatch him out from under his hopeful bride's nose."

They both giggled…cackled more like it.

Why…those women were no better than a pair of weasels, no matter how refined they appeared.

Lilleth must have gasped, probably loudly since she was quite rightly offended.

Both ladies turned to stare at her. How was it that in this posh hotel so many people had long noses which they used to look down upon others?

"I do not think the bride would appreciate hearing you say so," Lilleth pointed out.

The feathered woman arched a fine, thin brow and then laughed, but not with humor.

"Do you hear a buzz, Hilde? Come let's go into tea."

Clearly, those women had never been taught civility. Imagine speaking of stealing her future husband and not even bothering to whisper?

Shaking off their comment she moved toward the check-in counter.

A lovely melody from the violin drew her attention. This was one of her favorite pieces of music. She did hum this time, while walking toward the desk.

There truly were a lot of flowers. Fragrance swirled in the air and made the lobby smell like the rose garden at home.

What a strange sight it was to see trees in pots. Many

were palm trees she thought, although she had never seen one before.

She was mulling over how amazing they were when she stepped up to the registration desk.

"Howdy, Mister Gregory," she said, addressing him by the name he wore pinned to his jacket.

He stared at her for the longest time without speaking.

"Miss, if you go around to the back door, I am certain someone can help you with…well, whatever it is you need."

"What I need is my room and a bath." Normally Lilleth was the soul of patience but the attitudes of the people in this hotel were testing her goodwill.

"There is a hotel several blocks away in which I believe you will be more comfortable."

"If Viscount Aberly will be comfortable residing here, I will be, too."

The man gave her a deep frown. "How do you know he is staying here?"

Is…he'd said. Good then, her fiancé was already here. Once again, she was tempted to call upon his help but decided against doing so.

"It seems that everyone knows it, Gregory. I have traveled more than a day to get here and I would appreciate having the key to my room." When he made no move to give it to her, she said. "Please check the reservation for Miss Lilleth Younger."

Ah, that got his attention. The name Younger would be known to the staff since she and Mama were staying on the same floor as the Viscount…in the most expensive rooms the hotel had.

"Ah…um…welcome, Miss Younger."

She didn't feel welcome. She felt judged.

No one had ever made her feel less than worthy, and she did not care for the sensation.

Within a moment a young man came forward to carry her saddlebag. Not the rifle, though. It seemed wiser to carry it herself. There was every chance that the boy had never handled one before.

She followed him across the lobby. He stopped in front of a huge metal box attached to the wall. It had a door in the front and one in the back. The sides were formed of ornate ironwork which one could look through.

The boy opened the door then stepped inside the box, indicating that she should, too.

When she shook her head he explained, "It's only an elevator, Miss Younger."

Of course she'd heard of them but had never seen one.

"Are there stairs we can climb instead?"

"Yes, miss, but your room is on the top floor. This way is better." He smiled and it was the first friendly greeting she'd been offered since entering this palace. "Don't worry. I go up and down all day. It's safe…a bit of fun, too. You can see everything below. Bird's-eye view, it is. Come on in, you'll see."

The elevator had only risen about ten feet when there was a small commotion at the front door which distracted her attention from the odd sensation of rising off the floor.

Through the scrollwork she saw that a man had just come inside. People from all corners of the lobby rushed toward him.

Funny how they fell all over one another in an effort to see if he needed anything.

"That's Viscount Aberly. He's staying here. Folks make a big fuss whenever they see him."

"What's he like?" Who better to ask than someone who worked here.

"A real gentleman, I'd say. He treats the staff kindly and it seems like those little nieces of his like him real well."

Lilleth knew about the nieces. They were the children of the Viscount's late brother. The brother's wife had helped plan the wedding. It was her aunt, Deborah Newton, who was Mama's cousin from England.

The pretty box rose slowly higher giving her a unique view of the lobby…and the Viscount striding across it.

River Halston was a tall man. He had a purposeful gait which she admired, but that was about all she could make out of him with the elevator inching higher.

What she did see was the peacock-like women rushing at him.

She could imagine all too well how they were tittering and scheming to steal away her groom.

Then another woman crossed the lobby with three small girls bouncing about her skirts. Coming straight to River Halston, she embraced him. The little girls reached up for him clearly all wanting to be picked up at once.

It was sweet to see. But the best was when the schemers saw the embrace. They spun about, making their way back to the tearoom, she supposed.

Would this be her life, though? Women constantly trying to capture her husband's attention…even his heart?

"Here we are, Miss Younger. I'll show you to your suite."

It had been a long day and River Halston was relieved to collapse into a chair in his suite of rooms. It was perfect for all of them, with several bedchambers, a dining room, a drawing room and a small separate study that was tucked away.

Having resided in the same hotel during past visits to New York there was a sense of home to the place.

It had stretched his remaining funds to rent the suite for an extended period of time but he had no wish to have the children settled only to be uprooted again. It also saved money that any staff he required was supplied by the hotel.

The crossing from England to New York had been costly, too, with all that he'd needed to bring along. He might have conserved funds by renting a carriage and horses here in the city but he was getting married and the eyes of the most prominent people in both London and New York would be upon his family. He felt the need to put Aberly's best foot forward, so to speak. He had money enough to put on a show of prosperity until the wedding but no longer. Pray that nothing happened to interfere with the grand event.

River closed his eyes, listening to his nieces playing a game of some sort in the common room. He heard his sister-in-law, Clara, laughing at their noisy antics.

It was a good sound. Clara's laughter was something he had despaired of hearing again after Harold, his brother, died of the same fever that took their father.

What an awful illness it had been. It had swept through the family nearly taking them all.

Those had been wickedly dark days…followed by a hard year that nearly took him down, emotionally and financially. He hoped to never live through the like again.

Now here they were, not taken down. Because of Miss Lilleth Younger, they would soon be on the way up.

With his eyes closed, he let himself drift a bit, let his mind relax.

Being in public was often a trial, especially here in America. Anything he said was given more importance than it ought to have. It was as if he were the monarch and each word from his mouth a font of wisdom.

He was a man like any other, except that because of a title passed down through generations of Halstons, he bore the responsibility for the well-being of many people.

Everyone he loved, along with all who were dependent upon him would be left destitute if he did not carry through with this wedding to an utter stranger. A woman whom he had communicated with once, and that by a letter which Clara had declared to be no more than a note.

Time and again, he wondered what Lilleth Younger was like. Was her neat, feminine handwriting with its small loops and swirls an indication of her character?

She might be generous or selfish. She might be beautiful, or she might not. Was she easy to speak with or shy?

In the end it did not matter. She came with the wealth he lacked and so he would wed her.

While he enjoyed hearing the sounds of his nieces at play, in the moment he needed a quiet place to spend time before dinner.

Pushing up from the chair he went to the wardrobe, withdrew a plain coat, the one he wore in the hope that people would not know who he was.

This early evening, fall was in the air and the weather invigorating. Crisp leaves chased his boots while he walked across the garden.

Opening the stable door, he walked past a groom polishing a saddle then another groom leading a pair of horses out. There was nothing quite like a well-tended stable to soothe the soul. Earthy scents of horses and hay, along with whinnies and snorts all combined to put one's heart at rest.

Turning left at the last stall he came to another row of stalls where Aberly's horses were stabled. He'd brought his own groom with him from England. This was yet another expense he could not really afford, but he did not trust the care of his animals to a stranger.

"I'll finish brushing," he told Mr. Moreland. This was a task he found soothing and often performed at home.

The groom nodded then went into another stall.

With each stroke of the brush across the horse's glistening chestnut coat, tension drained from him.

It was no wonder he'd been on edge of late. In a week he was to meet the stranger he was to wed. While he hoped she would be kind…and in his heart he did hope for pretty, all she needed to be was a genteel woman with polished manners. Someone who would represent Aberly with grace and dignity.

But what was that? He paused mid-stroke to listen.

A woman was singing. Or an angel. Her voice filtering through the stable was so lovely it could be, either. He fancied the melody to be a lullaby, putting the horses to rest for the night.

He'd try and remember the sound in case he needed something soothing to help him fall asleep.

Which he probably would. Just because he was making a convenient marriage did not mean it set easy on his mind. Bringing a stranger into the family was a risky thing. What if she did not get on with Clara and the children?

Alicia had been amiable, but not really close to them. None of his family had wept when he… Well, never mind.

Past heartache and current worries faded while he listened to the voice of the angel-woman serenading the stable.

All at once he needed to know what she looked like.

Turning away from the horse, he went exploring.

Going down one row and then up another, he finally spotted her.

The lady appeared to be a servant. Her dress was of a common material and wrinkled. Which was odd. At home the servants were in uniform, always neat and tidy.

Also odd was that a maid would be in the stable. It was unusual.

None of that was his concern. All he wished for was to listen to her exquisite voice for a moment.

What a transfixing sight she made, stroking a horse's nose and singing to it.

He ought to make a noise of some sort. It wasn't acceptable to stand and stare. But it was the oddest thing—the troubles that had beset him lately did not feel as pressing.

Being rather absorbed in the moment he did not wish to speak.

Finally, good manners made it impossible for him to remain silent any longer.

"Good evening."

With a start, she swung her gaze at him. Her eyes grew wide, then blinked as if she were trying to determine if he was really standing there.

Even in the dim light of the stable he noticed how blue her lovely eyes were. How her cheeks were pleasingly round...and the sweetest shade of pink. This lady had an unaffected beauty that the polished women of his acquaintance rarely had.

"Howdy."

He could only liken her smile to sunshine, giving warmth and light all at once.

"I didn't mean to intrude." he answered, fighting an uncharacteristic grin.

Rarely did he allow himself to indulge in an unrestrained smile unless it was with his nieces or Clara. He did not wish to risk the recklessness that came with unguarded joy. Having lived with the consequences of indulgent behavior, he was careful, distant even, in his exchanges with people.

For all the risks of wedding a stranger there was a benefit as well. One could remain detached without it seeming awkward.

It had been a long time since he'd allowed himself to freely grin and would not do so now. However, his mouth did twitch because on the inside he was grinning. It took all his restraint to repress the gesture, but there was a quality to this pretty stranger which defied his best efforts.

To make a guess, the servant girl did not know who he was. He wasn't dressed like a viscount and he just noticed he still held the brush in his hand.

Maybe she would think him a stable hand.

It would be refreshing to speak with someone who was not attempting to impress him or discover what they might gain by an association with him.

What could it hurt to let down his wall for a moment and enjoy a simple, unguarded conversation?

It was as if the sweetest apple at the top of the tree just fell into Lilleth's cupped hand.

This was an opportunity like no other to get to know her future husband. Discover who he was before meeting him as her betrothed.

"I hope you do not think poorly of me for stopping to listen, but you have a lovely voice."

What a lucky thing he thought so. It would not do if he disliked singing since the urge to do so came upon her at times.

"I don't mind at all. I'm always singing and people are always hearing me."

"I was grooming a horse," he lifted the brush he gripped in his fingers as if to prove it. "I was drawn by your voice."

Already she'd learned something of value. The lordly Viscount did not count himself as too highborn to take care of an animal.

"This is Arrow. He likes being sung to. Poor boy is a little nervous with all the noise in the city. So am I." And that was the truth. This town, so full of strangers, amazed her but set her on edge, too.

Even this man she was to wed was a stranger. Hopefully not for long, though. She'd like to take this unexpected meeting to get to know him.

"You aren't accustomed to being in a city, then?"

"Not at all. I'm a country girl. I've never seen anything like New York before."

"I'll admit, it is quite something."

Seeing River Halston up close, she thought he was quite something, too. She was not going to mind seeing those green eyes looking back at her over the dinner table.

"Well then, I suppose I'll be on my way, but thank you for the song. It was quite enjoyable."

On his way! He could not go yet. She wanted to know more about him. She'd burn with curiosity the whole week long if she didn't.

"I was just to sing another song to Arrow. Sit and listen if you like." She nodded toward a hay bale along the back wall of the stall.

"I ought to get back." He lifted the brush, a reminder that he'd been brushing a horse.

"Yes… I suppose you must, but I'll be here this time tomorrow in case you'd like some company."

His gaze grew shadowed so she figured he was going to turn her down.

Hoping sugar might sway the moment, she gave him her sweetest smile. The very one that made Papa buy her a pony when she was four years old.

"Perhaps I will, Miss…?"

She could hardly tell him. It wouldn't be right to rob Mama of making their formal introduction. Besides, she was not ready for him to know who she was yet.

Saying she was Lilleth Younger would give her away quicker than a rabbit could hop from here to there.

"I'm Emily." And she was, this was her middle name after Mama's mother. "It's been a pleasure to meet you… Mr.?"

"Won't you call me River? And it was a pleasure to meet you, too."

With a nod and a smile, he walked away.

Watching him go, she got a curious flutter near her heart. His long bold strides spoke of a manly man. One who took control of life.

She supposed he would have to, having been born to responsibility as he had been. From what she had seen, people jumped to do his bidding in the hopes of befriending him.

Everyone wanted to be connected to dukes, barons, and the like, but only for the gain it might get them, was what she thought.

In her case it was different. River would be the one who gained from association with her.

Here was one more reason to get to know him before he realized who she was. As matters now stood, he believed her to be simply a woman he met in the stable so he might be his natural self in her presence.

The man she wished to get to know was the one beneath the weight of his title.

Please, oh please, let him accept her invitation to visit her here tomorrow.

The next day River again found himself with time between the afternoon's invitations and dinner.

Although he was weary from visiting, from performing his part as Viscount, he did remember one invitation…very well, not remember, it had been on his mind all day long.

The young woman from the stable had invited him to join her this evening.

There was something enticing about her, something that went beyond attraction to her pretty face and the beauty of her voice.

She seemed so natural in a world…his world, where posturing was an art form.

Perhaps this attraction to Emily had to do with her not knowing who he was. It was a rare moment when he did not have to be anxious that everything he said or did would be judged to a regal standard.

To Emily he was simply a man grooming his horse.

For a brief time he had let down his guard in her presence and smiled from his heart.

He ought to be concerned at letting it happen. But to his astonishment, the more thought he gave to the matter, the less concerned he became.

Very soon he would wed and probably never encounter Miss Emily again. A circumstance that meant that there was no time for her to tempt him to neglect his duty to the title in favor of amusement.

The lady was charming in a lovely, quaint way. Somehow during the brief time he'd spent with her, he'd not felt the sting of what happened with Alicia or the anxiety of wedding a stranger.

Had that been simply a moment out of time? A reaction to her song?

Possibly, but he had to wonder if that easiness of heart would come back if he saw her again.

Rising from his chair, he grinned. There was but one way to know for certain.

Before going to the stable, Lilleth visited the kitchen and asked to have a basket of food prepared. Somehow the staff had gotten the idea she was taking a meal to a recluse employer who disliked public dining. She did not correct them.

Not realizing who she was, they spoke freely among themselves. What an interesting moment that had been.

While Society folks could not get enough of Viscount Aberly, always posturing and fawning over him, belowstairs folks held a different view of her fiancé.

To them River Halston, while kind and respectful of the staff, was at heart no more than a fortune hunter.

Their opinion of her was worse.

Lilleth Younger was a title hunter, willing to give her wealth to a foreigner when she ought to wed an American and keep her money home where it belonged.

Now here she was, sitting on a bale of hay in the stable and waiting for the foreigner she was to wed and enrich.

There was every chance she was waiting in vain. He hadn't told her he was coming.

A loaf of warm bread in the basket gave off a delicious aroma. She was hungry and had half a mind to take a nibble while she waited.

But no, the bread was meant to act as a lasso to draw River in if he did pass by. No man she'd ever known could resist a meal, although they were mostly hungry ranch hands. She did not know if the same was true for gentlemen of high society.

Lords and ladies were called foreigners for a reason… they were foreign and their ways were often different.

Until she got better acquainted with River, it would be best to keep her identity to herself. If she was to give her life to a stranger, and she could do nothing else—she wished to know who the man was, not the Viscount.

Oh, but the scent of warm bread was the smell of home. It made her stomach growl and her heart ache. She loved Apple Valley Acres and feared that no place would ever have her soul like those vast acres of land and trees did.

Not that it mattered what she feared, she would go forward with her life.

"Where are you, River Halston?" she mumbled, fingering the corner of the cloth napkin and tempted to eat the bait.

Just in time she heard footsteps. Seconds later there River was, standing at the open stall gate and giving her the most appealing smile she had ever seen.

"Well, howdy, River. It's good to see you again."

"Hello, Emily. It's a pleasure to see you again, too."

But, what if he was only passing by on the way to tend to his horses. He had five of them; she'd counted on the way out of the stable last night.

"I stopped at the kitchen on the way here." She tossed her lasso. "I've got warm bread, cheese, and even apple pie if you'd like to share it with me."

She patted the space she'd saved for him on the hay bale, held her breath. *Come in, come in, come in*, she silently urged.

With a nod, he strode toward her.

My goodness but he was tall. As well muscled as any

horse wrangler, too. River Halston was a man to make a woman's heart tickle her ribs.

Now that she'd drawn him in, she needed to figure out what to say to keep him there.

"The hotel makes delicious bread. As good as at home," she said.

"And where is home, if I may ask?"

She couldn't tell him where, now could she? He might figure out who she was and then she wouldn't learn what she wanted to about him.

"Near Devotion Springs." Safe enough to say since few people knew of the small town.

As far as conversations went, this one was as dull as bones. She wanted to talk about him and learn more than what he had revealed in his letter.

"You've got an interesting name, River. I like it."

"Do you?" He took the piece of bread she handed him and made a sandwich with the cold cuts and cheese she'd opened. "There's a story to it."

"I'd adore to hear what it is."

He shrugged. "Very well… You could say my naming was my father's fault. He wasn't the most logical of men, forever looking for a merry time. The morning of the day I was born he decided it would be a good idea to take my mother on a long walk beside the river that flows through…" He paused as if deciding whether or not to reveal where he was from. She hoped he didn't because then she would feel obligated to be forthright about where she was from. "Through the meadow near where we lived. My mother objected, but my father insisted it would be great fun. As it turned out, that is when I decided to be born. When they came back from the walk my father was carrying my mother in his arms and my mother was carrying me in hers. So…they decided to call me River."

"What a unique and wonderful way to get a name. I was only named for my grandmother."

"It seems to me that's a better way to be named."

"Grandma Emily was a wonderful lady and I'm proud to be named for her, but there is no adventurous story to go with it."

"Do you enjoy adventure?" The frown etching compelling lines across his brow indicated he might not.

She had no idea why frown lines should be compelling but on him they were.

"Life is full of adventure whether a person wants it or not."

"That's a beautiful horse," he said, clearly finished with talk of his naming or of adventure.

"Horses don't come any finer than Arrow."

She stood up, humming a tune while she walked toward her horse.

Glancing back at River, she saw he was smiling, his eyes crinkled in good humor.

"Do you enjoy singing?" she asked. Perhaps they had something in common.

"I used to, but it's been a long time."

"If there is one thing this horse likes it's a good song. Come over here, let's sing to him together."

"It's been too long. I don't think—"

"Surely you do not wish to disappoint him?"

The urge to sing lurked behind the smile twitching the corners of his mouth. She was certain it was there.

"'Beautiful dreamer awake unto me…'" she began, hoping Stephen Foster's pretty melody, which skipped over her heart like a butterfly on sunflowers, would tempt him.

"'Starlight and dewdrops are waiting for thee; Sounds of the rude world heard in the day, Lull'd by the moonlight have all passed away...'"

She waited but he simply stared at her. Perhaps the hesitation had to do with him not being familiar with the words to the melody.

Then all once he grinned, laughed and caught her hand. He twirled her about as if they were waltzing. Then he joined in the song. He held her gaze...and the tiniest bit of her heart.

"'Beautiful dreamer, Queen of my song, List while I woo thee with soft melody; Gone are the cares of life's busy throng... Beautiful dreamer awake unto me.'"

Then at once he let go of her, his smile sagged.

"You have the most beautiful voice I've ever heard, River."

She'd gone so soft inside it felt like she didn't have bones.

"My father was admired for his voice." The subdued tone of of his voice suggested he was not proud to inherit the trait.

"Look at how Arrow enjoyed it. I do believe he would smile if he could."

"Does he belong to your employer...or your husband, perhaps?"

"Why, no. He is mine. I brought him from home when I came to New York...alone with no husband."

His brows drew together. Clearly he wanted to know about about her situation. Most likely he was wondering how a woman of meager means, which he and everyone else thought her to be, made enough money to own such a fine animal and keep it in the stable of this expensive hotel.

"You traveled alone? Forgive me for seeming surprised. Where I come from ladies travel in the company of others."

"That must be inconvenient for them."

Looking down at her gown, she thought of the ladies he must be speaking of. She would appear a dull brown mouse in comparison to them.

Tomorrow she would visit the banker and withdraw money. The purchase of a gown or two was in order. She was tired of being judged by her appearance.

Mama had told her to wear this gown so that she would go unnoticed in case she'd been followed. From what Lilleth had seen, in this hotel fancy gowns were far more common than humble ones were.

And yet she could not make a drastic alteration in her appearance since River already had it in mind that she was poor. Changing too much would raise questions.

Still, she would pay the store a visit. She'd get a new dress and hat, something more flattering than what she'd been wearing ever since she arrived.

She was weary of the arrogant doorman acting as if she had an odor every time she walked past him. It wasn't true, every night she took a long bath using the violet-scented soap which the hotel maid brought with the water.

"Tell me about your horse," Lilleth said feeling that a change in the conversation was called for. "I'd adore to see him."

"Very well." He nodded then stood.

Lilleth gathered the blanket she had spread over the hay bale. River picked up the basket.

Although River was not dressed formally like he'd been when she first spotted him entering the hotel, to her way of thinking he was even more wonderful to look at.

Compared to him, she was plain as dust. She did not wish for his impression of her to be drab. No one wished to wed a drab woman, compelled to do so or not. She was not dreary within her heart and so should not look as if she were.

Perhaps while shopping she would purchase two dresses in bright happy colors.

Lilleth had to look up at him while they walked along a row of stalls since the top of her head only came to his shoulder. At the end of the row, they turned a corner. The stable was as well maintained as the stable at home was.

"Which of them is yours?" she asked, wondering which of them he would show her.

"This one, her name is Morgan."

Ah, the smallest and prettiest. It was the one she had taken an instant liking to last night.

The mare in the stall beside Morgan's whinnied to River and nudged him with her nose.

"Hello, Morgan," she said, stroking the animal's sleek black forehead. "Aren't you a little beauty?"

"And gentle to go with it. It is why I brought her with me to America. She is like a pet to the children."

"You have children?" she asked knowing he did not. But she would dearly love to hear about his nieces who would become her nieces once they wed.

"Not yet. I was speaking of my nieces. I hope to have a couple of children one day, though."

"I'd like that, too, but we need more than only a couple..."

What had she said? Embarrassment blistered her cheeks.

"I hope you do," she scrambled to explain. "I mean... not us...together."

Mama had warned her time and again, not to say everything she thought of. Now she wished she'd heeded the lesson.

"It was nice seeing you, River. Maybe we'll meet again."

For now though, the sooner she was back in her suite of rooms the better.

"I hope we will meet again, Emily."

Maybe he did, but he wasn't smiling when he said so.

No doubt she had made a such a great fool of herself by speaking of children that he wished to never see her again.

If so, he would be greatly disappointed.

"Well, good night." With a nod, she spun about and walked away, picking up the picnic things and grabbing at shreds of her pride as she went.

Now that she'd humiliated herself beyond redemption, she could not bear to spend another moment with him.

Not until Mama arrived, bringing with her the gowns they had ordered, which were exquisitely appropriate for a viscountess.

When she and her betrothed were formally introduced, she would be wearing a regal-looking gown sent all the way from Paris, France.

Chances were he wouldn't even recognize her.

If she could just keep out of his way until then, he might not recall the girl in the stable he'd danced with, and laughed with. The one he had confided the story of his naming to...the one who had been so foolish as to speak of having children with a viscount.

Chapter Four

"You seem restless, River," Clara pointed out while River sat with her in front of the common room fireplace. The children were asleep so all was quiet.

His sister-in-law was correct. How could he not be restless when all he could think of was dancing and singing with a pretty and mysterious servant girl?

What he ought to be doing was giving his intended bride as much thought. It was only a day until she was scheduled to arrive at the hotel. Two days until the arranged meeting.

In the face of his silence Clara leaned forward in her chair, made a point of engaging his attention.

"It's understandable under the circumstances. I realize you have no choice in the matter but, really, a man should not be forced to wed. Especially a man like you. It breaks my heart to think of all you have to offer a woman. All that love in your heart gone to waste."

Love? Whatever love remained in his heart had soured when his beloved waved him goodbye without a tear. Her beautiful face, her smile and the sound of her voice had thoroughly beguiled him and now all that remained of it was a heavy heart.

How could Clara imagine he had anything to offer to anyone else?

"Love in my heart? Clara, I've never met Miss Younger."

She waved her fingers in dismissal of his statement. "But I have read her letter. She has remarkable penmanship, add to that what my Aunt Deborah has to say and…Do not look away, River…clearly you are making a brilliant match."

"It is brilliant, but do not mistake it for a love match. I am wedding her for financial reasons as you well know. If I had been allowed to wed for love—"

"Alicia? Really, River, surely you recognize that she was not meant for you. If she was she would be grieving, not expecting a child."

"What? Alicia is with child?"

The news should not hit him with the force of a blow. She was married…quite happily wed. And yet, Alicia was living the dream that was supposed to be theirs.

"It is a rumor which may, or may not, be true. The point is, you must let go of her and look forward to life with Miss Younger."

"Look forward? I accept it as is my duty. But understand, Clara, I do not look forward to this marriage and have no intention of offering my heart, not again."

"Dear, devoted River, where would we all be without your noble sacrifice?"

Clara had a way of speaking her mind which he found challenging…and endearing.

"I do not know why my brother married you," he said, smiling so she would understand the jest.

"Two reasons. Being second in line and only a spare son, he was free to do so. The other is that he loved me…and I loved him. I have every confidence you will give your heart to the lady you marry."

He might be at risk of such a thing if Miss Younger had sky-blue eyes and a smile that sparkled with intelligence and humor. He had not seen Emily in three days and was surprised at how much he missed her company.

The plain truth was, he did not want his wife to be like Emily since he had no intention whatsoever of falling in love and thereby making himself vulnerable to unwise decisions.

Perhaps had he not been so enraptured by Alicia, he would have noticed that his father was not paying attention to Aberly's financial condition. If only River had considered the adage that love is blind Aberly would not have come within a breath of ruin.

One thing was certain, he would not make the same mistake again.

The more homely and dour Lilleth Younger was, the better.

"I need some air." He rose to take a walk in the garden as he was fond of doing at night.

"Be careful out there." Clara did look worried.

"I'll be just downstairs. I'm certain its quite safe."

"Ha! Many a man has been trapped by a title hunter in the garden."

He had every reason to know it to be true, but that had been in England. New York was different.

Keeping out of River Halston's way meant hiding away in her room much of the day, tapping her fingers on the windowsill and gazing longingly out the window.

Down below a parade of life went by. There were wealthy ladies walking in groups or attached to the arms of gentlemen. She wondered if it was true that a lady was not allowed to walk alone in London.

It must be so or River wouldn't have mentioned it.

Three women walked past, arms linked and heads together in conversation. The hats the women wore were a fine source of entertainment. Surely they bore more feathers than the birds who gave them up would have had. If Mama had purchased any like them for her, Lilleth would pluck the feathers first thing.

Back home her family often entertained wealthy, important guests. Lilleth was no stranger to money and people of influence.

But it was different in the city than in rural Connecticut. Here there was so much wealth on display. It was nearly as if showing it off was the reason for having it.

Was London this way, too? If so, she was not certain she would fit in. She would do her best to perform as Viscountess but she was who she was and did not intend to become a person she was not.

A boy passed by below, calling out for people to buy the newspapers he was selling. The little fellow couldn't be more than five years old. His ragged clothes were far too big for him.

People flowed around him like he was a twig poking up out of a stream.

She could not be certain of his circumstances, but there was every chance he was an orphan, otherwise his parents would have him properly dressed and attending school. It was a lucky thing she'd visited the bank and made a withdrawal. Tonight this child would have a warm meal and a new set of clothes. Hurrying downstairs, she decided she must also find him a good orphanage to live in if that is what he needed.

It didn't take long to catch up with him. His dirty face and hands cut her heart to the quick.

"I'll take all of your newspapers," she said, then handed him ten dollars, which was nothing to her but would be everything to this little one. "Do you need a safe place to stay? If so I will help you find one."

"Thank you, ma'am." He sneezed then wiped his nose across his sleeve, all while stuffing the money in his pocket.

"Come along with me." When she reached for his hand, he dashed away through the crowd of wealthy shoppers, none of whom seemed to notice.

Supporting orphans in Devotion Springs had been a far easier task. Children did not just run off into a crowd. Possibly because there was not a crowd to run off into.

She wasn't acquainted with River Halston well enough to know how he felt about children living in poverty, but she would insist her money be used to help children like this newsboy.

Back in her rooms, she noticed that eventually the sun went down and the streets emptied of shoppers. Carriages went by below taking fancy ladies and gentlemen to the opera, the theater and maybe even a ball.

It could be that River had gone out, performing some important viscount business. If so, it would be safe to go out of her room.

With darkness fallen, it would be a pleasant time to walk in the garden…but what if River was not away from the hotel?

He might also be walking in the garden.

It might be wiser to gaze up at the sky from her window.

What a comfort to see the stars and the moon and know that the same ones were shining down on Apple Valley Acres.

Earlier this afternoon River had gone to the stable but did not find Emily.

There was no reason for him to be disappointed. What he ought to be was relieved.

He thought of her far too often. The lady of humble circumstance was not meant for him.

And a very good thing she was not.

It would be foolish to deny that the inclination to indulge in frivolous behavior was within him. For all that he wished it wasn't, there were times when it was hard to cling to a sober, sensible attitude while in Emily's presence.

Standing still while his valet dressed him for dinner, River grinned inside. He could not summon a sober thought while remembering how Emily's face and neck blushed when she'd spoken of having children and she'd believed he interpreted it to mean their children.

The woman was a delight he could not afford to indulge in, as temporary a delight as it would be.

He would not go to the stable again unless it was to visit his horses.

If he never saw sweet and spicy Emily again it would be for the better. His heiress was due to arrive tomorrow. He was to meet her the day after.

Miss Emily, whose last name he did not even know, was not his future. Miss Lilleth Younger was.

Later that evening he attended a formal dinner with the elite of New York Society in the hotel dining room. It was a long affair and two hours into it he began to feel stifled by the attention being pressed upon him.

He longed to get out, to stretch his legs in the garden.

With a whisper to Clara, he rose and left the other diners staring after him.

One person took special interest in his departure. Her gaze rested upon him far too pensively. River knew the look too well. Miss Mulligan was not the first woman to set her sights on his title, but hopefully, she would be the last.

One good thing about being wed was that the risk of him being compromised into marriage would be eliminated.

Brisk autumn air cleansed him of the stuffiness from the close quarters inside. He stood still for a moment listening to leaves rustling in the breeze. Cool fingers lifted his hair with the sensation of a whisper.

Thinking of fingers lead to a vision of Emily tracing the white blaze on Morgan's nose with her small, pretty fingers. What, he wondered was the lovely servant doing this moment?

"Curse it," he mumbled. "Get your thoughts in order, man."

Just because Emily was not married did not mean she could...What? Become the mistress he did not believe in taking?

Quit her job and take employment from him where she would constantly tempt him to smile...or even laugh aloud?

To dance with her in his arms without a care?

He must take a care!

Frivolity was the road to ruin and he would not walk down it.

All at once he heard a moan.

Hurrying around a tall bush where the path curved, he discovered Miss Mulligan, the woman from dinner, sprawled on the stones, her gown ripped from the neck to the shoulder.

Unless someone had actually attacked her, he'd fallen into a trap and no way out.

"Unhand me you villain!" she screeched up at him. "Someone help me!"

He cursed aloud, not caring who heard him.

With only a week until his wedding, he'd been caught. Snared by a woman who would probably bring nothing into the marriage but misery. Being forced to wed her meant utter destruction to everyone who counted upon him.

Again he cursed the moment he decided to venture out by himself and the misguided reason he'd done it. Which had not been to take the air as he'd told himself, rather he'd gone out hoping to encounter Emily.

Wasn't this just proof that bad things happened when one allowed pleasure to have its way?

"I am sure you cannot be speaking to me, miss," he stated in a futile attempt to extricate himself from this trap.

"Why, you villain! It is only the two of us here and so you thought you could assault me like some common—"

"Howdy, River."

Stepping out from what seemed to be nowhere, Emily shot him her sunshine smile. Then she stabbed a severe expression at the woman trying to tug her torn dress in place.

"Like some common liar, as I see it. What a pitiful thing to do. Accusing Viscount Aberly of attacking you when you are the one who attacked yourself. I cannot recall ever witnessing such poor behavior."

Miss Mulligan gathered her skirts and stood up.

"Who are you to question me?"

"Why, I am the very one who heard you tell your friend to hide in the bush and then pop out when you screamed for help. I'm the one who saw you rip your dress like it didn't cost a dime, and then sit down on the path to wait like a snake in tall grass."

A bush rattled close by. Footsteps tapped the path indicating the escape of the false witness.

"You should go now," Emily advised. "You would not wish for news of this to spread."

The woman threw Emily a haughty glare.

Miss Mulligan made a shooing motion with her fingers, seeming to shrug off the insult.

While Emily watched the woman dashing away, all River could do was look at his rescuer. How did one properly thank someone who had just saved him and everyone he loved?

Emily rocked back on her heels, crossed her arms over her middle. "Humph…it would be fitting if everyone knew what she did."

It also seemed fitting that he should take her in his arms and kiss her…out of gratitude.

He lifted his hand toward her with every intention of doing so. But then, looking at her smile fade, seeing the sudden awareness of what he had in mind dawn on her… then knowing in a flash that it was not gratitude he would be expressing, he dropped his hand, curled it into a fist.

"I'm getting married," he muttered.

"Yes, I know."

With that she caught her skirt in her fists and dashed away.

Lilleth would have preferred riding Arrow to the train depot to meet Mama but decided the horse would be more comfortable inside his peaceful stable.

In the name of blending in with New York Society, Lilleth hired a fancy carriage like those she'd watched drive past her window. Mama would appreciate a comfortable ride. Hopefully she would not mind that Lilleth had purchased a new gown from Lord & Taylor yesterday.

The plan had been to look as plain as possible until her mother arrived, which was now. It could not hurt to arrive at the station looking like a lady.

And the truth was, Lilleth appreciated feeling dressed

up. Ruffles circling her wrists, the gown's nipped-in waist, along with the dainty shoes she'd bought in a shade to match the gown, they made her feel like she was attending a party at Apple Valley Acres.

As lovely as it was, this gown was simple compared to the ones Mama was bringing with her.

While sitting on the cushioned seat of the open coach and watching more people than she had ever seen in one place walk in and out of the doors of the train depot, she thought about what a marvel this city was.

New York was a place of wonder. There was something interesting to be amazed at everywhere a person looked.

A clock the size of a carriage wheel mounted on the front of the building struck three o'clock. One of the trains she'd heard blaring its whistle behind the building was likely to be Mama's.

"I'll be back shortly," she informed the driver.

He stepped off his perch then came around to help her down. With a polite nod, he promised to wait.

It was interesting what a fashionable gown could do to improve people's manners.

Making her way through the crowd toward the area where she would meet her mother, Lilleth saw some plainly dressed ladies and some fancy ones. Naturally the fancy ones caught everyone's eye. Each woman she walked past looked more glamorous than the next.

It was a lucky thing that River was marrying her for her fortune and not her elegance.

What, she wondered, would he think of her as his viscountess. He liked her as plain Emily and that was who she was at heart.

It had not escaped her attention…had utterly captured it, in fact…that he'd considering kissing her last night.

It was a lucky thing he hadn't looked at her in that heated, speculative way for a second longer. She might have leaped upon him and given him the kiss they were clearly both imagining.

Wouldn't that have ruined Mama's plans for their elegant and proper meeting? Not to mention, she could not have pressed herself tight to him without admitting who she was.

Thinking about it now, she might have been wrong not to tell her fiancé who she was from the first. River was bound to be stunned when he made the discovery.

But he'd gotten to know her as much as she'd gotten to know him, which could only be for the best.

"Lilleth!"

Being lost in thought, she jumped at the sound of her mother's voice.

"Mama!" She wrapped her mother in a great tight hug. "I missed you so much. Where is John?"

Glancing about she did not see the tall, slim figure of the farm manager.

"He's arranging for the trunks to be delivered to the hotel. I am so relieved to see you. Has everything gone well? I can't tell you how worried I've been. Oh, but look at you! There was no need to worry at all. Clearly you have met with the banker. What a lovely gown. And those shoes…!"

"I went shopping at a store called Lord & Taylor."

"I know of it. In fact, I bought my wedding gown there before your father and I eloped. Which I am happy you are not doing."

"Now you can have the wedding you wished for through me, Mama."

"No, dear. It isn't that at all. Or not much. I did have the wedding I wanted. You know I was never sorry for marrying your father."

Lilleth nodded; she did know. Her parents had loved each other deeply.

"But I believe Papa is looking down and smiling at how things are turning out. He did want you to have, again, the life you gave up."

"I never could convince him that I did not regret my decision to live in America. He felt such a need to make it up to me. It was why he earned the fortune he did. Although I do miss England and Society sometimes, I would never trade that life for the one I have now."

Lilleth hoped she would come to feel the same way about her life in England. The difference for Mama was that she had been in love with Papa.

While she could not quit thinking about how exciting it would be to kiss River, it certainly did not mean she was in love with him.

She was only just getting to know the man.

"Ah, here comes John." Mama linked arms with her. "Let's go prepare you to meet your viscount. Tomorrow will be a grand day."

"Yes…about that, Mama…"

Lilleth sat at her dressing table watching in the mirror while the maid's fingers twirled her hair in loops and whirls. With a dash of flourish, she added a ruby-studded comb behind Lilleth's ear.

Looking at her reflection this way and that she decided she looked like a work of art more than a woman.

A casual hairstyle was what she was used to. Elegance was what she must get used to.

"Thank you," she said.

The maid looked over her handiwork, gave a satisfied smile then gathered her tools and went out of the room.

Lilleth's nerves were strung so tight she figured she might unravel the pink bow securing the front of her silk corset.

She turned on the stool to look at her mother.

"I imagine Lord Aberly will change his mind for certain once he knows what I did."

"I doubt he'll recognize you," Mama said with a laugh then turned to the gown hanging on the wall and fluffed the skirt.

The dress was beyond beautiful, far too lovely to wear to her execution…or to tea as her mother called it.

A single rap tapped on the door. Deborah Newton entered, sailing across the room to embrace Mama.

They spoke for a moment about the grand adventure they'd had this morning exploring shops and spending time together.

Next, Deborah turned her attention to Lilleth, her smile as wide and pleasant as the rest of her was. The lady, Lilleth was certain, was one of those people who became one's bosom companion upon first meeting.

"Why, our little bride is every bit as enchanting as you told me she was, Mary. I can't wait for dear River to meet her."

"Oh, indeed," Mama answered. "It is bound to be a memorable moment."

And shocking. But this was a problem which was no one's fault but her own. Whatever came of her small deception she would have to deal with the consequences.

Having set out at the beginning to discover whether or not she liked her groom, she found that she did like him quite well. She only prayed that she had not ruined any chance of them having an agreeable marriage.

A marriage in which the kiss he had nearly given her would happen…and happen often.

While gazing in the mirror and watching light from the window glimmer in the jewels of the comb, she grew rather warm.

If she became so heated over an imagined kiss, how would she react to a real one?

"River, my dear," Aunt Deborah said while patting his arm and looking earnestly up at him. "There is no need to be overwrought. I have met your bride and she is quite lovely."

He was fond of the lady he called Aunt, although she was not actually his aunt, but he did not completely trust her judgment on the matter of whether Miss Younger was lovely or not.

It was a rare person that Deborah Newton did not find lovely.

"I assure you, Aunt. I am not overwrought."

Nervous though, as was to be expected.

The meeting was to take place here in the tearoom of the hotel.

For privacy sake, the tearoom was closed to all but the few who were invited.

Those few being Mrs. Younger and John Dalton, the manager of Miss Younger's horse ranch.

The man, he'd been informed, was a longtime friend of the family and had insisted upon standing in the place of Miss Younger's late father.

On River's side there was Aunt Deborah and Clara.

Although they were quite excited for it, the children

would meet their new Auntie Lilleth at another time and place.

Before the girls were presented, he needed to know that Miss Younger was a woman who tolerated small children. Not all ladies did. Some were nervous around them and he would not subject the girls to her resentment if that were the case.

For all that he'd adored Alicia, her smile at his nieces had never been all that genuine.

There was a knock on the tearoom door. His nerves jumped but he put on his stoic, viscount demeanor.

It turned out to be only a pair of maids delivering tea, which meant the moment of meeting would soon be upon them.

"Oh, lovely! Thank you, my dears," Aunt Deborah said to the maids.

Nodding and smiling, the young maids left the room, passing by Clara coming in.

"What a beautiful afternoon," Clara declared. "We have looked forward to it for ever so long."

"There's a storm outside, in case you failed to notice," he grumbled because everyone seemed so cheerful without even knowing what sort of woman they were adding to their small family.

"Oh my, it seems to me there is one inside, too. If I were you, dear brother-in-law, I would put on a happier face. Unless I miss my guess, your bride will be coming through that door any instant now."

"How do you come by this guess, Clara?"

"I came down the elevator with Mrs. Younger and her daughter. I hurried ahead to warn you to smile since I knew you would not be."

Smile…he really ought to. He gave the gesture a go but

was rather certain by his sister-in-law's frown that he was grimacing.

"Never mind, River. I hear footsteps in the hallway."

The door opened slowly, inch by inch. John Dalton entered first then stood to the side while Mrs. Younger came in.

He did not see the daughter, only the hem of her gown in the corner of the doorway. Apparently, she was hesitant to enter the tearoom.

"Come in, Lilleth," Mrs. Younger urged.

The portion of the gown visible in the corner of the door frame remained perfectly still.

"Excuse me, my lord," Mrs. Younger said and then stepped into the hallway.

"I am certain all will be well," he heard the lady assure her daughter.

Hopefully his bride-to-be was only having a fit of nerves. Pray that she was not stubbornly balking at having to wed.

It was not too late for Miss Younger to change her mind. The possibility made his gut cramp.

Clara was right, he should smile. He must not scare the young lady off with a less than welcoming expression.

Mrs. Younger came back inside, her cheeks round and blushing in pleasure…and pride, it looked like.

The ruffled hem of the gown caught the light and shimmered with a forward step.

Miss Younger appeared in the doorway.

His first impression of her was that she small and well formed. He could not judge if her face was as lovely as her figure because he could not see it.

Miss Younger was staring at the floor.

Taking what appeared to be a steadying breath, the lady

looked up. He had the oddest sense that he seen her before. Her eyes were as blue and pretty as—

As Emily's.

"Howdy, River."

She'd be happier if River would smile.

Although Lilleth could not blame him for being flummoxed, he didn't need to look as if he'd been stung by a hornet.

"I realize I'm late in doing so," Mama said, not seeming a bit put off by River's frown. "But please let me introduce my daughter, Lilleth Emily."

While she had not expected him to take the news without a bit of shock, being face-to-face with his stiff attitude riled her.

She was the same woman he'd eaten bread and cheese with in the stable, the one who shared an admiration of horses.

Indeed! The very one he'd nearly kissed.

Only two days ago she'd rescued him from ruin and now he acted as if she were the ruin.

It was on her tongue to point out that she was the one keeping him from said ruin.

Then a quick glance at Mama reminded her not to voice every thought that crossed her mind.

"You've already met?" Clara, whom they had just come down in the elevator with exclaimed, clapping her hands and smiling. "How wonderful!"

At least someone thought so, even if it wasn't the one who ought to think it.

Everyone was looking at River, probably waiting for him to utter a gentlemanly greeting.

It was a good thing she already knew a thing or two

about her intended, otherwise she'd mistake him for a bear woken from hibernation too soon.

Had this stern-faced fellow been all she knew of Viscount Aberly, she would be discouraged.

Luckily, she'd learned there was another side to him.

"Forgive me, Emily…rather… Miss Younger. You've taken me by surprise."

"You're entitled to a bit of a sulk," she admitted. "I suppose I'd be in a mood too, if I were you."

"I assure you, Miss Younger, I do not sulk."

"Well, whatever that look is on your face, I apologize for putting it there."

"Oh, look! Little sandwiches…don't they smell delicious?" Deborah exclaimed. "Mary, dear, would you like to pour tea?"

"Oh my, it has been a while since I performed pouring in the proper way. But yes, I would enjoy it."

Seeing her mother looking so delighted put a smile all the way to Lilleth's soul.

If making her mother happy was the only reason for marrying River, she would do it. Everyone at the ranch had lived through dark days after Papa's death, but Mama most of all.

No price was too high to pay in order to see her mother sparkle once again.

It was a premature thought since she had yet to speak her vows, but once grandchildren began to arrive, Mama would be forever smiling.

"Come, now," Clara touched Lilleth's sleeve. She snagged River's elbow. "The two of you sit here at this table in the corner and get acquainted…or better acquainted as it is. I'm certain you have a great deal to discuss."

It seemed that River did not want to discuss anything.

He sat silent as a stone in the chair beside hers. It was a relief when Mama handed them both a cup of tea and a plate with two tiny sandwiches on it so that she could pretend to pay attention to something other than stretching silence.

Conversation had never lagged between them before.

She decided not to be the first to speak but rather turned the sandwich in her fingers, looking at it and not him.

"I apologize for behaving churlishly," he said, giving her a sidelong glance.

"I apologize for not telling you who I was." She slid a sidelong glance back at him. "It's just that I wanted to know who you were…as a man not a viscount. A girl doesn't marry a stranger every day, after all."

"No? It's fairly common where I come from." He glanced at her full on but then quickly away.

"Maybe, but it's not common for you any more than it is for me, no matter what other people do."

"I suppose you are right. Still, I would have appreciated knowing who you were before now."

This time she looked at him without glancing away.

"You do know me. I am the same person you met in the stable and so are you."

"I hope you find me acceptable given that you've had a few days to think it over."

"I do find you acceptable." The corner of his mouth twitched but she could not say it was a smile. "And I'd rather marry you than Coulder Snell any day of the week."

"I'm flattered." He ate the sandwich in one bite. "I was informed there was threat to you, but not the specifics of it."

"I suppose you should know. I do not expect further trouble from anyone in that family, but one cannot predict what they will do when they discover I've escaped them. I imagine they are spitting fire by now."

"They would have harmed you?"

"In order to get Papa's land and fortune? Yes, they would. Last week, had I not been warned that they meant to take me by force to marry the eldest son, Coulder, I would not be here now." River drew in a breath, probably realizing that his own future had also been at risk. "It was a narrow escape. I rode for New York in the dark of night. It is why I was here earlier than planned and dressed as a servant. Mama wished for me to be disguised. She feared that once they knew I was gone, they would follow."

He took her hand in both of his and gave it a squeeze. His expression serious and, she thought, protective.

"Rest assured, Miss Younger, you have nothing to fear from them any longer." After another squeeze, he gave her hand back.

Lilleth took a long sip of tea, but it was not the liquid warming her. It was knowing that there was a big, bold viscount standing between her and the Snells.

"Thank you, River. It is a great relief to me…and not only me, but Mama and everyone back at the ranch."

Finished drinking tea, she set the dainty cup aside.

"I like coffee better," she told him. "But I suppose there are things I'll need to get used to. However, having you call me Miss Younger is not one of them."

Chapter Five

Howdy, River… Sitting in his chair River went over in his mind the moment when two words changed his future.

He was not to wed a woman he was indifferent to after all and he found the prospect disturbing.

It didn't matter that right now three-year-old Violet was tugging on his sleeve begging him to play horse and rider… the image of Emily standing in the doorway looking like an angel in blue satin could not be scrubbed from his mind.

But she was not Emily—she was Lilleth and, despite what she had said about knowing her already, the lady was a stranger to him.

Of course, he'd been expecting a stranger so he couldn't understand why he felt betrayed.

"Take me on a ride, Uncle River, pleeeease!"

Although his mind was miles from playing horse and rider, he stood, then picked Violet up and settled her across his back.

"Talley ho!" she called and he began to gallop about the room.

One could not be betrayed by someone one didn't know, he reminded himself.

But what she'd said was actually true, he did know her.

And there in lay the trouble. Having believed he would

never see Emily again, he had allowed his true self to emerge, had revealed a part of himself to her that, ever since Alicia, he'd kept buried under a heart more stone than flesh, so to speak.

Now that Lilleth had seen that part, he feared he would not be able to take himself back.

She would expect him to smile and be merry. It was not who he was any longer.

"You're going too slow, Uncle River!" Violet kicked her pretend spurs into his sides. "Make a horsey noise!"

"Neigh!"

"My turn!" Elizabeth and Victoria both cried out at once.

Violet tickled his ear, making him laugh.

Very well, sometimes merry was who he was.

However, he would not be merry with his wife.

Dashing around the room and getting winded, he understood why he'd appeared "surly" earlier.

Lilleth Emily Younger was one of the cheeriest people he had ever met. His hopes of wedding a lady of serious demeanor were dashed.

He'd been anticipating, or hoping for at any rate, a lady of sober refinement. One who knew her duty as Viscountess and would perform it without requiring anything of him in the bargain.

The future Lady Aberly posed a threat to his state of mind. If only she had not made him laugh. Worse, made him dance and sing.

How was he to maintain his mental sobriety when at every turn she tempted him to act like the man he used to be with Alicia?

He did not dare to be vulnerable, and yes, irresponsible again.

No matter the temptation, he meant to keep that man buried.

Perhaps a trip to the stable was in order. A visit with his horses was sure to set his emotional balance to rights.

"I'm going out, Mama."

Lilleth's first meeting with River as her fiancé had not gone well and she needed a few moments of solitude to think it over.

If he would not even call her by her name, how were they to get along in their marriage?

Since there was no backing out for either of them, it was important to find a way forward.

"Surely you are not going outside. It's raining."

"I enjoy rain, you know I do. And I have some things to think over."

"I suppose you do, dear, but have you a rain slicker at least?"

"I'll buy one first thing in the morning, although I think the ladies in New York are partial to dainty umbrellas."

"Have I been away from Society so long to forgot that? We shall both purchase umbrellas tomorrow although slickers are far more practical."

Lilleth kissed her mother's cheek then grabbed a pair of apples from the table. Then she snatched up her wool coat and out she went.

Rain tapped her cheeks as she dashed through the garden. The cobbled path was wet and reflected the light of dozens of lanterns, which illuminated the way.

It appeared as if she was dancing along a path scattered with diamonds. The magic of the moment lifted her spirits at once. A lively tune came into her head. At first she hummed it, but then she sang it aloud.

Once inside the stable she took off her boots. They were wet and cold. She placed them next to the door rather than carrying them.

Oh, but the stones were icy! Dry, though.

Someone else had recently come in out of the rain for wet boot prints marked the floor. It was not surprising since stablemen went about their business at all hours and in all weather.

Continuing her song, she made her way back to Arrow. Singing was a good way let her joy rise, to keep it from being dragged down by her gloomy groom-to-be.

She felt for the apples she'd slipped in her coat pocket as a treat for her horse.

Hmm, not in there. She walked slower looking down at her skirt and searching the pockets to see if she'd put them there.

All at once she bounced off of something. She gasped, the song stuck in her lungs.

Of all the bad luck, she had ricocheted off the one person she did not wish to see.

Although, she ought to have guessed River would be here.

Seeking peace among horses was something they apparently shared.

"Good evening, Miss Younger."

She shook her head, gave him a stony glare. He was not the only one with the ability to look stern.

"Good evening, Lilleth," he corrected then stepped a few paces backward. "What brings you out in the rain?"

"I imagine the same thing that brings you out." Digging in a pocket she found the apples. "Here, give this one to Morgan."

"You should give it to her."

Perhaps this was his way of acting cordial so she smiled and said, "I would enjoy making friends with that sweet mare."

"She is good-natured. My nieces have their pick of horses but they always choose Morgan."

"How many horses have you got back in London?"

"Oh…well there are those I keep at the town house… then more at the country estate outside of London. To be honest, I don't know how many."

"It must have been a worry for you, not knowing how you would keep them fed," she said then wondered if she should have.

He might not wish to discuss what had happened to force him to marry a…What was it she was called? Oh, yes…a Dollar Princess.

After a very long moment, he replied, "It was."

"Between us we should have a respectable-sized herd," she commented, deciding it was better to speak of the future rather than stirring past hurts. "What is your place in the country like?"

Green like Connecticut, she hoped. She'd seen paintings of English meadows that looked lush and peaceful… something like home. Not as cold in the winter, she'd heard that, too.

"The estate in England is different than what you are used to. Nothing there makes a profit. It's more a place for the family to get away from the bustle of London. I think you will enjoy it."

It was reassuring to hear him include her as one of the family. This time next year she would be living an ocean away from everything she knew and loved.

The choice she'd made was a costly one, because she was not only handing over her fortune, but her future as well.

She could not have made another choice and would not change it. Regardless, she would strive to have a friendly relationship with River Halston. She would win him over if she could.

"I'll warn you, though, it's not always peaceful in the country," he said drawing her back to the conversation from which she had thoroughly wandered. "We are required to host house parties. Guests from the city often stay for a week. I dislike the endless entertaining, but Clara adores it."

Although he had said "we" she did not know if he meant her and him…or him and his family as it was now.

"Life in England will be far different than you are used to." For an instant the expression in his eyes changed, going from guarded to vulnerable. "I hope you do not regret agreeing to this marriage."

"It wouldn't do me any good if I did…but the truth is, I don't. New paths open up in life and it's up to us to choose to walk them in joy or in misery."

Hearing him agree with her would have been encouraging, but he kept his opinion of what she said to himself.

Surely though, he agreed. Anyone would.

They arrived at the stalls where the Aberly horses were housed.

"Why, hello, Morgan. Aren't you a sweet girl?" She fed the apple to the horse. "Why are you frowning at her, River, she is a sweet girl. You said so yourself."

"I wasn't frowning at the horse."

"Then why are you frowning at me?"

"That's not…" There he went looking flummoxed again. "I'm not frowning at you. It's more the situation we find ourselves in."

As she suspected, he was walking their new path grudgingly, not with joy.

"River Halston, what good does frowning do? Things are what they are. You'll go bankrupt without my money and without your protection, I'll probably get kidnapped. As I see it, we can consider ourselves victims of fate, or we can consider ourselves allies."

"That's a positive way to look at it." He raised a handsome eyebrow at her, but she couldn't tell if he agreed with her.

"Being allies is a good start since we can't expect to be a proper husband and wife right off. That will take time and getting to know one another. Bonds of the marital nature are not formed at once."

"Are you always so straightforward?"

"Mama warns me not to say whatever crosses my mind. But I say, what's the point of pretending you think something you don't? Or don't think something when you do?"

"The point is that you might not want for everyone to know every little thing about you."

"Yes, but we aren't talking about everyone right now. This is about you and me."

River turned his attention to the horse in the next stall, clearly not wanting to have this conversation.

Since it was an important one, she pressed on.

"I already know who you are, River, so why hide behind gloom and doom?" She gave Morgan a slow stroke down her white blaze then spun on her cold bare feet and walked the hallway toward Arrow's stall.

"Gloom and doom?"

River was forced to take long strides to keep up with her because even though she was the soul of joy most of the time, she did become irritated upon occasion.

"Being sober minded rather than frivolous is not the same as gloom and doom."

Her coat was beginning to feel cold from being damp with rain so she shrugged it off while she walked. When they reached Arrow's stall, she draped the coat over the rail.

The horse whinnied so she fed him the apple.

Sensing River standing behind her, she turned to look up at him.

"I am not lacking in cheer," he insisted.

He was not lacking in masculine appeal, either. Her insides turned buttery imaging what it was going to be like to kiss his lips into a smile…as a wife would have a right to do.

Her irritation slipped away.

"The man Emily knew was not, but the one Lilleth knows? All I can say is it's a good thing I met you first as Emily. I know the truth about you, River Halston."

"What truth?" he asked, the words spoken cautiously, she thought.

She countered his mood with a smile. "I know who you really are…and I like you."

Lilleth liked him?

How could she like a man she did not actually know? Curse him for letting her see as much of him as she had. Now look what had come of it.

He would need to be more wary in the future. Her playful attitude put him off-balance, made him want to respond in kind…to laugh and smile. Perhaps indulge in a flirtatious wink.

The last thing he could be was the man she thought she knew. He had struggled to put that part of his character to rest and would not resurrect it.

He reminded himself that there was one reason he was marrying this woman and that was to fulfill his duties as Viscount.

One of the duties was to produce an heir. He winced inside because the word *produce* sounded as unfeeling as ice.

Until recently he had not expected to beget a child out of anything but love.

Produce though…as unfeeling as it seemed, when the time came that was all it would be.

With a glance at his soon-to-be bride, he was not sure how he would manage keeping his emotions out of the act, and yet he must.

He only wished that Lilleth was not so appealing. But then he might easier to wish that stars did not twinkle.

This woman was everything a man could wish for.

Except that she was not Alicia.

And that would be the very thing to keep his emotions out of the marriage bed.

But Lilleth liked him. Her wide blue eyes sparkled when she said so.

What did a man say in the face of such a revelation?

This woman was no stranger passing through his life whose sentiments could be casually dismissed.

He must respond in some way.

"It is reassuring to know. It is best for allies to like one another," he said then wished he could call back the words.

What a foolish, insensitive response. He ought to have told her he liked her, too. It would not be a lie.

"It is also wise for allies to know some things about one another," she said seeming to challenge him with an arched brow.

When he remained silent, she said, "I will begin."

Without a moment of hesitation she did.

"My parents knew everything about each other. They were an odd match in some ways. Papa was so big and bold. Mama was, and still is, all about proper manners. At the same time she is strong. My parents didn't always like what they knew about each other, but they sure were in love."

In love? Hopefully she did not expect the same.

River regretted seeking peace in the stable. All he'd found was anxiety.

Love was the last thing he envisioned in his marriage as well as the last thing he wished to discuss.

"My parents also loved one another, but to the exclusion of everything else. My father all but forgot he had an estate to run. And here we find ourselves because of it."

"Don't look so dour. I don't expect a declaration of love, but I do expect for us to be friendly with one another."

"I'm sorry, Lilleth. You are completely right. I shall endeavor to be more cordial."

Lilleth shifted from foot to foot, looking uncomfortable.

"Is there something wrong?" he asked.

"My boots were wet so I took them off and now I'm cold all the way up to my eyes."

Which meant she was probably in her stockings under her skirt. He jerked his imagination away from wondering if her feet were as shapely as the rest of her was.

His coat had dried out so he shrugged out of it and placed it about her shoulders.

Quite by accident, or by a careless move, or perhaps by… never mind why…but his fingers grazed her neck.

She quit shivering.

A chill quaked through him.

Not that he was cold. Heat from touching her crept up his fingers, lifted the hair on his forearms then singed the vicinity of his heart.

He had an urge to draw her close when what he needed to do was back away. He was far too close to indulging in a detrimental whim.

"Ask me to marry you," she whispered. "You never did that."

On one knee? That was a romantic gesture. This marriage was not that.

She must have read his thought because she laughed. "I don't need flowery poetry, only the words to make this all feel real."

Very well, he need not go down on his knee, but some gesture was needed. He took her hand, telling himself they were partners casually shaking hands on their arrangement.

Curse it though, no business partner had hands which were all at once capable and strong…small and warm.

"Lilleth Younger, will you do me the honor of marrying me?"

Those words hit him smack in the heart in a way he hadn't expected them to. He tried not to, but he got lost in the soft expression glowing in her eyes.

"Yes, River, I will marry you."

And then while he was held by her smile, she placed her hands on his shoulders and rose to the tips of her toes.

She kissed him.

It was a brief glide of her lips, not much more than a rush of warm breath on his mouth, but when she started to settle back to her feet he needed more. He gripped her elbows drew her in for a deeper kiss.

He touched her hair…trailed his fingers down her small slim back.

It could hurt nothing to exchange a kiss during a marriage proposal. It would be expected.

But Heaven help him if he trod this path again once this moment was over.

He set her away more gently than the anxiety twisting his conscience accounted for.

After what he'd just done, she might expect for this to be the way of their marriage.

Friendly, not intimate, is what he intended. After feeling that kiss run him through he understood now, more than ever, this was a line he dared not cross again.

"Very good, now we are properly engaged." She blinked up at him, shrugged deeper into his coat then clasped it about her throat.

She looked quite small and vulnerable, although he did not believe her to be vulnerable.

What she was, was his to protect…not to love.

While Lilleth posed before the mirror in her chamber, dreamily recalling the kiss of the night before, a maid prepared her for her first public appearance as the future Lady Aberly.

Although the outing would appear to be a casual ride through Central Park, it was anything but. The point of taking the air in Aberly's open carriage…brought all the way from London…was for people to see her in it.

To judge her was what it amounted to, but she supposed this was to be expected when one was engaged to a viscount.

Funny to think how only days ago she'd been judged for her common dress. Life was awfully odd sometimes.

"Lilleth, my dear, you look so beautiful." Her mother hugged her tight. "I can scarcely believe we have come to this moment. So much planning between me, Deborah and Clara, and all the while with an ocean between, and here we are at last."

"Thank you, Mama. I appreciate everything all of you did to make my wedding special," she commented while turning in the mirror and taking a glance at the back of the dress. It really was very nice. She was going to look as good walking away as she did coming forward.

"Here, my lady, let me attach your hat," the maid said.

It was going to take some effort to get used to folks addressing her by a title that was not *Miss*.

This was only the beginning of the changes that she must get used to. While she would do her best, naturally, she had no intention of being who she was not, not at the heart of her.

Lilleth Younger from Devotion Springs was the title most dear to her.

Several soft knocks sounded on the door, coming from a spot under the doorknob.

The door opened and Clara came in smiling while herding three little girls before her.

"The carriage has been brought around and the girls are quite anxious to go for a ride. However, they are more anxious to meet their new auntie."

Lilleth was not certain she could bend down to greet each of the eager children. However nice the effect, her corset was strung so tight it was all she could do to breathe.

Elizabeth, she learned was seven years old, Victoria was six, and the youngest, Violet, was three and clinging to her mother's skirt as securely as a cocoon to a twig.

"My dear sister," Clara said giving her a hug with all three daughters crowded in between. "You look so elegant that you will be the envy of every woman in New York."

"Will Uncle River finally fall in love, Mum?" Elizabeth asked.

"Well, you know your uncle—I suppose he'll put up a fight about it," Clara answered. "But your new auntie is as beautiful as a princess and he will be smitten for sure."

Given what happened in the stable last night, Lilleth

hoped he had some interest in her that way because she certainly did for him.

The moon would turn green before she would quit feeling that kiss. She had never had her heart go perfectly still and then suddenly gallop like a runaway horse before. It was a wonder that she'd gotten her breath back at all.

And the touching had not ended with the nice long kiss.

Afterward, he knelt down in front of her and said, "Give me your foot."

When she lifted her skirt and extended her stocking-clad foot, he'd rubbed it briskly between his palms. Nothing had ever felt as delightful as his hands drawing the chill out.

For all that his expression had seemed gruff, his touch was no less than a caress.

After a few moments, he took off his boots and placed them on her feet.

They were still warm but also large and heavy.

She had not taken two steps before she stumbled.

"Hold on to my arm." He extended his elbow.

Gripping tight, she clopped toward the stable doors.

River grumbled something about not wanting for everything to be ruined by her perishing of pneumonia…which she was rather certain could not be caused by cold feet.

Touching him, feeling the heat and strength of his muscular arm, well then…she was in no danger of catching a chill.

Grumpy attitude notwithstanding, River was behaving as gallantly as any hero she'd ever read of in a novel.

It might be that he was only concerned about losing her money, but his hands had lingered longer than they might have while warming her feet. Indeed, he could have shoved his boots at her without touching her.

By the time they reached the back door of the hotel,

River had placed his arm over her shoulder and drawn her close to his side.

Wasn't it fascinating how a man who was not wearing his jacket or his boots could radiate so much warmth?

She'd grown hot as a blister and it had nothing to do with wearing his coat and his boots but rather being snuggled against his big solid form.

The unique sort of heat which pulsed from the man to whom she would soon be bound to in marriage was not one that a woman easily dismissed.

Her future groom seemed to be resistant to being close to her that way—surely his attitude would change once they wed.

After the way he'd kissed her, she knew he was tempted.

This was one bride who was not giving up without a fight.

Lilleth was known to be determined. Mama always believed it was her tenacity that had kept her from dying when she was three years old and struck down by a horrible fever. Although Lilleth did not recall the situation, Mama claimed she, herself, had never recovered from the ordeal.

Motherhood was as strong a devotion as the Good Lord ever created. She'd seen the bond in both animals and humans. When that precious time came for her, she hoped to be as fine a mother as her own was. And to give Mama many grandchildren to help ease the ache of the children she'd lost.

In order for that to happen she must have River's cooperation. And not only in the physical matter of getting their children conceived, but also to love them and be a cheerful influence.

One way or another she meant to unearth the man who had laughed and danced with Emily.

Chapter Six

The coach was filled with females. To River's eye, ruffles, bows and colorful bonnets made the open-air conveyance look like a vase overflowing with flowers.

Lilleth sat beside him smelling so good he could barely concentrate on autumn's beauty turning the trees shades of amber and rust.

He didn't know what a Connecticut horse ranch smelled like, but he imagined it was Lilleth scented…a combination of fresh air and wildflowers. And warm lips…a scent which surely only lingered in his memory.

If Lilleth was aware that people were staring at her, it was not apparent. She was clearly preoccupied with getting to know her nieces and might not realize she was being evaluated.

Even if she did know, he'd discovered his fiancée to be a courageous lady who was not easily daunted. And a good thing she was not since the judgment she faced in New York would be nothing compared to what she would encounter in England.

When he returned home there was bound to be gossip about his bride, perhaps even subtle hostility.

While he had not left anyone believing he would court them, there were many who had made it their life's ambition to be courted. The affront of him giving the title of Viscountess to an American would not be easily overlooked by the British noblewomen who coveted it.

"Shall we stop and let the children play by the fountain?" Clara suggested.

Since the girls were bouncing back and forth between the seats, it seemed a wise idea.

"Would you mind?" he asked Lilleth, because sitting in the carriage was one thing, but getting down and mingling among curious people was quite another. "If you wish we can remain here while the children expend their energy."

"I've got some energy to expend, too," she told him.

Only after he'd helped her down from the carriage did he wonder if she knew to call him Lord Aberly in public. He did not wish for her to feel embarrassed for not understanding the formality of British customs.

For now, they were in America so it did not matter so much, but when they went home it would matter a great deal.

He was surprised at how protective he felt of her.

Although why should he be surprised? Hadn't he given her his boots last night in the worthy name of preventing her feet from getting chilled?

The truth was, protective wasn't all he'd felt. In spite of the fact that he was wedding for necessity, he'd definitely reacted to the way her small, curvy body fit so well against his last night when he'd held her close to keep her from stumbling.

As much as he tried to pretend the kiss he had indulged in was merely friendly, he could not quite manage it.

What a fool he'd been not to anticipate the attraction.

The evening before, battling strong temptation, he'd

made some idiot comment about not losing her money to pneumonia.

What a thoughtless thing to say. It would appear as if he had a heart of stone.

It was going to be a daily battle remaining indifferent to Lilleth. What he must keep in mind was that he was not in a battle with her, but with himself.

The responsible side of him was at war with the imprudent nature he had inherited from his father. That very nature had made him reckless when it came to Alicia. Like his father, he had been so enraptured he couldn't think of anything but her. When it all came down upon his head, he been beaten and bloodied, the pain and the shame, raw.

Life had turned him into a wary man.

He had hoped for a woman who would be content to shop and entertain, one who did not demand anything of him but was satisfied with the social position which came with her marriage.

Lilleth Younger was not that woman.

As far as he could tell, she did not care about social position and would be happier riding her horse than riding in his distinguished carriage.

What mattered most was that she fit in well with his family, which she clearly did. He was quite relieved at that.

While walking behind Lilleth and Clara, watching them laugh and chat as if they had been sisters all their lives, he was glad that his bride would have a friend once they went back to England.

Clearly his nieces adored her. They took turns holding her hand and skipping along beside her.

Good then, his family was giving his wife what he dared not.

Namely, their hearts.

He was fond of Lilleth, was helpless not to be.

Fond was an emotion he could accept. There was a vast difference between that casual feeling and being in love and reckless.

Good Lord help him to never be in that state again.

"A puppy!" Victoria shouted.

Victoria chased the small brown-and-white creature around the fountain, its bejeweled collar winking in the bright sunshine. The pup did not appear to be concerned at being lost, which it clearly was.

"It's mine," Violet exclaimed, then joined the pursuit.

The tiny spaniel dashed in circles around Lilleth's skirt.

Lilleth knelt, made kissing noises and reached her hands toward the playful creature.

After one more romp around her skirt, it stopped to sniff her fingers.

"My puppy!" Violet cried, reaching for it.

Lilleth stood, bringing the pup up with her. Holding it close to her heart, she stroked its short nose. Then she touched her nose to a floppy ear and breathed in deeply.

"Nothing quite like the scent of a puppy, is there?" she asked him.

If he'd ever smelled one, it had been so long ago that he'd forgotten. "Possibly. I would not know."

"River Halston, do not tell me you have never held a puppy and taken a good sniff of puppy breath?"

"I do not recall the occasion."

"That is a sorry state of affairs, if you ask me."

Lilleth lifted the puppy to his nose. "Go ahead. Take a good deep sniff."

Unable to avoid doing so, he breathed in. Soft fur tickled his nose.

"Prince!" A woman called, her voice a bit frantic. Three other voices echoed the worried call.

"I think we know who little Prince belongs to," Lilleth said.

"To me!" Violet cried.

"And us!" called his other nieces.

"We must hide him in our skirts," Victoria instructed.

"He's as cute as a button but don't you think that would be unkind? We must give him back to his owner. It is the right thing to do," Lilleth explained as they walked toward the woman.

Clara bumped his arm with her elbow, gave him a knowing nod.

They followed because Lilleth could have no idea who was hurrying to retrieve her lost pup.

"This little fellow must belong to you." The dog's tail wagged madly when Lilleth set Prince in the woman's elegant, beringed hands.

"I cannot thank you enough. I would have been distraught beyond comfort to lose him."

River had met this lady a time or two and knew her to be gracious.

His nieces turned dramatic frowns upon the puppy thief.

"But he's mine." Violet's lower lip trembled.

"They are convinced that finding him is owning him," Lilleth explained.

"Well, young ladies, I will always be in your debt. And especially yours, Miss Younger."

Lilleth shot River a questioning glance.

"Oh, my dear, of course I know who you are. It is not every day that a Viscount comes to New York to wed. It is quite the event. Oh, but please do let me introduce myself. I am Mrs. Astor."

"Howdy, Mrs. Astor. It's a pleasure to meet you and your sweet little Prince. And please do call me Lilleth."

"It's a pleasure to meet you too, Lilleth. And again, my thanks to you and these lovely children."

With that, Mrs. Astor and the group accompanying her continued on their way.

"Is that lady a queen?" Violet asked, looking after Mrs. Astor, her expression caught between resentment and awe.

"New York does not have a queen, my darling," Clara told her. "But if it did, Mrs. Astor would wear the crown."

River stood next to Lilleth, both of them gazing after Society's queen and her companions.

She slipped her hand into the crook of his arm so naturally that it caught his heart before he had a chance to erect a defense.

"She seemed friendly."

"Mrs. Astor is known for being gracious," he told her.

"You have made a wonderful ally, Lilleth," Clara said. "You could not have made a better one…a circumstance which other women are bound to resent. Not everyone makes the acquaintance of Mrs. Astor, although everyone wishes to."

"I imagine it is only because she knows I'll soon be Lady Aberly."

Lilleth stood in River's cozy parlor looking at rain pattering the window and listening to the children involved in some sort of game.

At a table in front of the fireplace Mama, Clara, and Deborah, played cards.

A storm had come in late yesterday afternoon and grown worse ever since. It looked as if her wedding day would be a wet one.

While she watched, wind swept sheets of water down the street. Fashionable carriages did not crowd the road; no one strolled about to see and be seen as on a normal day.

Fashionable folks and common ones had the good sense to shelter inside.

All except for that one fellow. She watched him step down from his coach and dash toward the hotel's front door. He carried a large box with a red bow on top.

"Don't fall off the couch," Lilleth heard the eldest of Clara's daughters, Elizabeth, advise with a great deal of urgency. "The sea monster will get you."

"Has he very large teeth?" Victoria asked, excitement in her tone.

"Not as big as mine," this from little Violet. "I shall eat him before he gets you."

Violet's older sisters praised her bravery.

Lilleth only hoped to be so brave. This time tomorrow she would recite lifelong vows with River and, she'd been told, all the best people of New York Society would be in attendance.

The only people attending that she knew were Mama and John Dalton, Clara and her girls along with Deborah, and her new acquaintance Mrs. Astor.

Most important, of course, was her groom.

On a normal day he looked tall and impressive. She could only wonder what he would look like tomorrow with his titled finery on full display.

Lord and Lady Aberly were bound to shine.

The gown that served as her titled finery hung from a hanger back in her dressing room.

If anyone from home saw her picture in the newspaper, they would not know who she was. She'd had some very nice gowns over the years, but this one came from Paris, every detail of design dictated by Mama. Clara and Deborah had given approval for the placement of every jewel and crystal sewn into countless yards of fabric.

The gown had been nearly a year in the making and tomorrow she would put it on, along with the title of Viscountess.

Before she could slip too deeply into worry over how she would perform in that exalted role, a loud rap punched the door.

Even though the Halstons were staying at a hotel, they had a butler. Mr. Gordon hurried from a side room to answer the door.

"A delivery for the Misses Halston from Mrs. Astor," announced the man she had watched dash into the hotel moments earlier.

He handed the box with the red bow to the butler.

The box tipped awkwardly in Mr. Gordon's hands so he set it on the floor.

Sea serpents and card game forgotten, everyone gathered around, staring at the red bow which was jiggling.

River came out of the small office where he had been going over his correspondence, seeming as curious as the rest of them.

While they all peered down at it, the lid of the box shifted then slid off onto the rug.

A black puppy with a white face hopped over the edge wagging her white-tipped tail.

All three children screeched. The noise must have startled the poor little pup because she deposited a puddle on the floor.

Clara swept up the dog before her deliriously joyful daughters could snatch it and further frighten it.

River slipped a card from under the bow.

"'Please accept this gift in appreciation of rescuing Prince,'" he read to them all. "'She is his littermate and I know she will find a lovely home with you. With best regards and sincere thanks, Caroline Astor.'"

"She is mine?" Violet asked with tears dotting the corners of her lashes.

"Yes, darling." Clara patted the top of Violet's head and smiled that special smile that mamas had when they were watching their children's joy. "Yours and your sisters. You shall share this gift equally. Now, sit on the floor in a circle so she can sniff you. And while she does you may choose her name."

Mr. Gordon cleaned up after the dog while River inclined his head toward Lilleth, indicating a bench in the bay of the window having a view of the rain-lashed garden.

Lilleth followed and then sat beside him.

"It was kind of Mrs. Astor to reward the girls with a puppy…did you notice how good it smelled?"

"It isn't as if I had a chance to get near enough. My nieces are over the moon."

"You have a nice family, River. Since I was born it was only me, Mama and Papa. Then it was only me and Mama. Except for John, he's like family."

"Tomorrow that will change. My family will be your family, too."

"I'll be a viscountess," she muttered, fluttery nerves getting the best of her.

"Are you ready for it? This will be a different life than what you are accustomed to. If you wish to change your mind you must do so today."

And leave him and his family financially ruined? Clara had confided that it had taken most of their funds to come here in the style which was expected of a viscount. She simply could not, nor could she return home unwed.

"No, River, I do not wish to change my mind. I love the ranch, but my life isn't there any longer. There is a new road opening for me. I'm not sorry about it, but I do think it will take time getting used to. I am accustomed to working. Although, I never considered caring for our horses to be a chore. Every day had a purpose to it. From sunrise until sundown there are animals to be cared for as well as the hands and their families to be provided for. I will miss it."

"My mother used to say being Viscountess looked easy, as if her life consisted of paying social visits and being admired. But it was all hard work."

"I know how to run the farm, River, but Viscountess? I won't know how to act."

"Clara will help you…and your mother will for a time."

Yes, for a few weeks, until she and her new family sailed for England and she left her mother behind.

How would she and Mama get by without each other? It was not as if her mother could just move to England with her. Apple Valley Acres still needed someone to run it. Although once she wed it would belong to River and so be his responsibility, but it was for all purposes still Mama's farm.

Lilleth was going to miss her mother beyond words. Could she really become a mother herself without having her own Mama close by to help?

Right then she had the urge to run back to Devotion Springs…but in that instant a big warm hand closed around her fingers and squeezed.

"It will be all right, Lilleth."

It was true. In time things would surely work themselves out.

She had a husband-to-be who was a near stranger…but

many women had worse. A vision of Coulder Snell's mean-spirited grin flashed in her mind.

It was a great relief knowing she was safe with River.

She squeezed his fingers in return, smiled at him, but he was staring at raindrops pinging the window so did not return her smile.

While being Viscountess for the vanity of social position was not important to her, there was something which was.

And that was having a husband who smiled at her, one who shared life's common joys.

River did not need to love her. Not yet. Circumstance had brought them together, not mutual affection or even attraction.

Although, it would be a great fib to say she was not drawn to him.

He had not let go of her hand and the sensation was oh, so pleasurable.

Still, it took two willing people in order to form a love bond and at this point, all they had was a financial bond.

Glancing over at the rug, she saw that at least one love bond was growing on this stormy afternoon.

Tiny Morganette, as the girls were calling her, had already captured the hearts of everyone.

Chapter Seven

Trinity Church was filled with people braving the weather in order to witness Viscount Aberly take a bride.

While he did not turn to look at it, the huge stained-glass window behind him would be illuminated with each lightning strike stabbing the city.

He was far too anxious to pay attention to anything but his bride who would be making her grand appearance at any second.

Mrs. Younger walked down the aisle then took her seat in the first pew of the church.

Aunt Deborah was escorted to her place in front.

Next, his nieces carried their flower baskets walking, or skipping really, close behind Clara.

The next person to come down the aisle would be his bride.

His ally…and his foe of sorts.

Not that she intended to be his foe, only that he worried she would claim more of him than he could give.

His greatest fear in the moment was that seeing her, knowing that this woman was his to honor and protect, would make him experience emotions he had forbidden himself to feel.

He'd known a friend or two to actually shed tears seeing their brides coming toward them. Although they had been in love and he was not, the moment was bound to be emotional.

Taking a wife, for whatever reason, was one of life's monumental moments.

Music swelled announcing the moment to be at hand.

Bracing his heart for the instant she appeared in her white gown turned out to be useless.

At first sight of his viscountess gliding toward him as if in a frothy cloud, seeing her cheery, hopeful smile…he was undone. How did men who were in love with their brides get through this?

When he took her hand to escort her up the steps to where the reverend waited, she winked at him.

Everything was conspiring against him. The church, seeming all the more intimate because of the weather outside and the smiles on the faces of the women in his life…the striking beauty of his bride…it all pushed him to feel things he did not wish to feel.

After the vows were finished and the moment came for him to kiss his bride, he was so caught up in the romance of it all that when he lifted her chin, lowered his lips to hers, he whispered "Lilleth" so intimately it was as if he was giving her his heart as well as his name.

He was not doing that. He could not…later he would need to make sure she understood that this was simply a moment out of time.

Their marriage would not be built on romance…although just now with her lips under his, even briefly, it did seem like it.

A great cheer filled the church.

He held her hand while they turned to greet the guests. Even that touch squeezed his soul.

They were now Viscount and Viscountess…husband and wife.

* * *

Lilleth was a married woman. A lady of high society.

Her wedding was a bigger occasion than she had ever imagined, even though she'd been told it would be.

Riding away from the church she peered through the carriage window to see people huddled under umbrellas along the sidewalk. Lined two and even three deep they stood in the rain just to get a glimpse of the aristocratic newlyweds.

"I can't believe they came out in the rain," she said. "I hope no one gets sick. Should we stop and thank them? Maybe encourage them to go home?"

"A friendly wave of your hand will do."

"I suppose you are used to this sort of thing."

"Born to it. But don't worry, you'll get used to being watched."

"Maybe, but it's awfully strange and I can't imagine I'll like it."

However, shifting her gaze from the window to her groom, she could imagine liking something. Kissing her husband. She'd had two kisses already and was developing a fondness for them.

In spite of having hundreds of people in attendance, and despite the fact that she and River were not in love, the women of her family had planned a wedding that was intimate…romantic.

The morning had been so much more than she had expected. Even her groom had appeared emotional which was unlike him.

If she slipped from her side of the coach to his, would he kiss her again?

No way of knowing unless she gathered her courage and did it.

She caught up her big billowing skirt and shifted across to his seat.

As luck would have it, the carriage hit a bump in the road and she ended up on River's lap.

Maybe he would not think it funny, but she found it hilarious that yards of white lace engulfed him and she could see no more than the top of his tall black hat.

He batted and swatted, giving the impression he was drowning in her wedding gown.

When his face came into view, looking stern, possibly offended, she began to laugh.

Lilleth was not certain she had ever been in a more humorous situation.

She drew her petticoat away from his chin.

"Do not tell me this is not funny. I defy you to deny it."

"That is because you are not the one up to your eyes in fluff."

She felt him trying to lift her away, but not being able to see anything, his fingers brushed the bodice of the dress.

"Forgive me," he grunted, clearly not appreciating their first intimate touch as husband and wife.

As unintentional as it had been, his touch kicked Lilleth's heart into her throat.

She swallowed hard, looking at his expression and realizing that his heart had not kicked.

Certain things did take time and patience she reminded herself.

"Accidents do happen," she said while gathering her skirts and shifting back to her own side of the coach. "There is nothing to forgive."

"It was a beautiful wedding," he said, probably trying to make amends for acting annoyed when there was no cause to.

"It was, thanks to my mother, Clara and Deborah." With her Parisian gown neatly arranged about her, she leaned forward on her elbows. "Now that all I have belongs to you, we need to have a discussion about it."

Clearly, he had not expected this turn in the conversation. He opened his mouth as if to say something and then closed it again, shook his head. "Right now?"

Since kissing was not what he wished to do, then yes, speaking of something practical would fill the time during the ride back to the hotel.

"I think there is no better time."

Although he was frowning, she thought it a handsome one. What she also thought was that, as his wife, it was her challenge…her duty even to turn his frowns into smiles.

"I promise to be diligent in caring for your money. I do not take the responsibility lightly."

"It's what you wrote in your letter and I appreciate that. But we must discuss a few matters face-to-face."

"It may not appear so, since you wed a man on the brink of bankruptcy, but I am dedicated to building upon the wealth you have bequeathed me."

"Again, I appreciate that. But please understand that I will have some say on how the money is spent."

"Do not think I am not grateful for all you have done to save the family. You will have a generous monthly allowance."

Allowance? The word felt like a dismissive pat on the head.

She crossed her arms over her middle, her temper beginning to rise. It was an effort not to accuse him of treating her like a child with no experience at managing money.

Back at the ranch the bookkeeper was not the only one with eyes on the funds coming in and going out. As soon as she'd understood arithmetic she'd watched at her father's elbow while he worked with the accountant.

"Allowance for what, River?" she asked mildly although she did not feel mild, which was a shame because it was her wedding day and a romantic ceremony only just completed.

At least for her it had been romantic, but there was no indication that her husband thought so.

"All the pretty things that ladies occupy their time purchasing. Hats?" His brows arched, hers lowered. "Gowns? Gifts for the staff?"

Gifts…indeed this was closer to what she had in mind… gifts to charity! Providing for orphans and the needy.

Finances were not something they had discussed beforehand because there hadn't been much time between meeting him as Lilleth and marrying him. Had she brought up the matter earlier, what difference would it have made then? They would have wed regardless.

But it mattered now.

She would argue, point out the error in his thinking, but the carriage arrived at the front door of the hotel and the doorman was hurrying toward them with an umbrella lifted to shelter them on the dash from the carriage to the big brass-framed doors.

Lilleth did not seem her cheerful self, although River could not quite understand what he had done to irk her.

Only moments into their marriage and they were at odds over something that he imagined would be revealed once they were alone in his…no, now their suite of rooms.

It would take some getting used to the idea that his life was no longer his own in many ways.

Lilleth's belongings were to be brought over within the

hour while they attended the wedding luncheon in the exclusive dining room downstairs.

A feast worthy of Queen Victoria was prepared for the wedding guests, the Astors among them.

Between now and then he must discover what was troubling Lilleth and do what he could to make it right. She would need all her natural cheerfulness to make it through the luncheon. He doubted if she had ever attended anything quite like it.

After a quick dash through the rain, he led his bride toward the elevator with photographers snapping pictures along the way.

The young elevator operator greeted them with a sincere grin.

"Congratulations, Mr. and Mrs. Aberly!"

What the boy lacked in knowledge of the proper way to address them, he made up for in genuine good wishes. If everyone they encountered from here on out was as sincere in their congratulations, River would not mind being called Mr. Aberly.

"Thank you, Billy," Lilleth answered.

"We appreciate your good wishes, lad," River said, drawing a coin from his pocket and handing it to the boy.

Cupping Lilleth's elbow he escorted her to their suite of rooms.

"Welcome home, Lady Aberly." He infused his voice with cheer hoping to ease her mood.

"It seems strange," she muttered but did not elaborate on the comment.

"It's strange for me too, Lilleth."

"I suppose we've got a lot of learning to do about being married. It's not like we were in love and can just fall into life as if we were."

What he did not say was that, had he been in love with her, he would not have wed her.

Love was something a man was better off without. It ended in heartache…at least for him it had.

Apparently, it had not for Alicia.

Giving himself a mental kick, he nearly groaned. He would not dwell on a former love on his wedding day.

"I have something for you…a commemoration of the day."

While not a romantic statement, the ruby and diamond necklace was a suitable wedding gift.

He indicated that she should sit in a chair while he went to his chamber to get the gift.

Lilleth now had every right to follow him into his chamber, but he did not invite her in. She might take it as a sign to freely enter whenever she wished.

"I don't think I can sit, not in this gown. You will recall what happened in the carriage."

As if he could forget. In one miss-aimed touch his bride had become all he wanted and all he feared.

When he came back to the common room he found her gazing out the window at the rain.

She spun about, distress shading her eyes.

What he ought to do was ask her what the trouble was. Since it was probably him, he did not.

Instead, he handed her the gift which was certain to bring a smile to her face. Any lady would covet such a prize.

Even the velvet box was a work of art.

He nodded for her to open it, anticipating the delight that would replace her troubled expression.

She lifted the lid, smiled and said, "It's pretty, River. I thank you for it."

And then she closed the lid with a snap.

"Earlier we were speaking of my…allowance, you called it?" She placed the box back in his hands, then returned to the window, tapped her finger on the glass. "I met a little boy selling newspapers a few days ago. I imagine our images will be on the front page of his papers tomorrow. But, River, what do you think he is doing now? A young child out in the weather?"

He knew of exploited children who sold newspapers. They were on London streets as well.

"Life is hard for many children," he answered, ashamed that he had given the needy little thought today. He'd been absorbed in his wedding and how his own life was being impacted by a woman he was finding ever more appealing.

"I think he is going without food, maybe without shelter and there are many more like him," she said, then after crossing the room, she touched his arm, looked up at his face. Her smile was pressed thin…sad. "The necklace is beautiful and I thank you for it…but the children… If you do not mind, I will sell it and use the money as a donation to local orphanages. Also, there is a place back home I wish to send money to as well. I understand that you are the one in control of the funds—it's how things work in your world which I have agreed to be a part of. But in this, I will have my way. I will have a say in how our money is charitably spent."

What was a man supposed to say to that, especially when he completely agreed with her on the importance of charity, especially when it came to the plight of children.

Unable to speak for a moment he simply started down at her beautiful stubborn face.

What sort of lady would give up this expensive bauble?

The one he married, was who. Clearly, she was not going to be refused in this, nor did he wish to refuse her.

What he wished was to kiss her.

"Very well, Lilleth." He covered her hand where it still pressed his arm, in entreaty perhaps but more likely insistence on getting her way. "I will sell the necklace and you will have full authority over spending the funds."

"Thank you, River. It's an acceptable start."

"You are welcome...but what do you mean 'start'?"

"I have no doubt that you will be a reliable steward of the money I brought to the marriage, but you do not know about what goes into running the ranch."

"I have spoken with John Dalton. We will deal quite well with one another. It is agreed that he will be my eyes and ears at the farm. I have given him and your mother full authority to act in my stead."

"John is a good man and reliable as daybreak, but I've been working with him and my papa from the time I was fourteen years old. I wish to have a part in the farm's finances."

"I do not doubt you are capable, Lilleth, but your life as Viscountess will keep you too busy for much else."

"Busy spending my allowance, do you mean?"

"Yes, that and receiving callers, paying visits...advising Cook on menus and helping the housekeeper oversee the staff."

"Sounds dull as bones to me, River. I might be a viscountess of a different sort than you are used to. I'll try my best to do those things you just mentioned, but I will also have a hand in the affairs of the ranch."

Looking into her determined blue eyes, he would never have guessed the Emily he'd met in the stable had such a willful streak to her nature.

Nor would he have realized how attractive that trait in her was. For all her petite size, she was strong-willed.

Strong-willed and tenderhearted…a combination of characteristics he would need to guard his heart against.

"I will not be denied in this."

"The ranch is your birthright. I agree to sharing the running of it with you. But about the allowance… I am afraid you must be seen spending Aberly funds. As Viscountess, you will set an example. Other ladies will shop where you do. The merchants depend upon our support for their livelihoods."

"Dull as bones," she repeated at the same time the door opened and the ladies of his family rushed in, all speaking at once.

One thing he knew for certain.

Life from now on would be anything but dull as bones.

Chapter Eight

River thought the wedding luncheon was a great success.

The guests in attendance appeared genuinely happy for the bride and groom. Perhaps some were only following the example of Mrs. Astor, but for the most part Lord and Lady Aberly appeared to be accepted by New York Society.

It would be interesting to see how they were received when they returned home to London.

Now, though, the celebration was finished and Lilleth had retired to the chamber which used to be Aunt Deborah's.

This being Lilleth's wedding night, no doubt she was nervous and wondering what came next.

He must pay her a visit, attempt to explain how matters would be between them and then depart before he changed his mind about how matters would be.

It was going to be a difficult night, knowing what he might have with her and yet sleeping in his own chamber.

Had she put on a seductive gown in anticipation of his visit? Was she sitting upon the bed ready to greet him with a smile and welcoming arms?

If so, how would he react? Would he give in to temptation or would he act as he'd decided he must?

Perhaps he was a fool to hold himself back from her. He

would need an heir at some point. Tonight was as good a time as any to try and accomplish the goal.

Perhaps get the…the deed…over and done with early on and then be free of the…

How big of a fool was he, anyway?

Lilleth he knew to be a woman of warmth and passion. She was a lady who would give herself freely to the man she loved. Although this was not the case between them, the kisses they had shared spoke a great deal of what could ignite between them.

He did not believe she would turn him away.

Dressing in his night robe, he crossed to the door separating his chamber from hers.

He rapped lightly on the wood.

Hearing no expectant call for him to enter or no demand for him to go away, he opened the door slowly then peeked inside.

Lilleth was not dressed in an inviting gown. She was not sitting upon the bed waiting for him with a smile and open arms.

His bride was asleep with the bed covers drawn to her chin and her golden hair spread across the pillow.

If he'd ever seen a lovelier sight he could not recall when.

He sat down on the edge of the mattress simply gazing down at this woman who was now his wife.

It was understandable that she was exhausted. It had been a long day, her first as Viscountess and she had performed the part amazingly well.

Probably because she was not artfully playing a part, she was simply being herself. It could not be denied that Lilleth had a natural charm about her which others were drawn to.

Now that she was Viscountess would other people watch her, emulate her? Since she was asleep, he allowed himself to laugh softly, wondering if upper-class New Yorkers would begin greeting one another with "Howdy."

Watching the covers rise and fall with her easy breathing he could not decide if he was relieved to find her asleep or disappointed.

Both, he realized, and that disturbed him.

Coming in he'd not intended to stay, but what would he have done if he'd found her awake and waiting for him?

Sitting here, looking down and seeing her lips twitch in her sleep, hearing her soft sigh, confirmed the fact that achieving the goal of an heir would not be as matter-of-fact as performing the deed of marital duty.

It was impossible for his heart not to be involved. One thing he was not, was indifferent to Lilleth Halston.

Even the simple fact that she now shared his name touched him, made him want to bind her to him.

However, what he wanted to do and what he needed to do were not at all the same thing.

As a newlywed husband, the want pressed, tempting him to draw the blanket down then gently awaken his bride with a kiss.

He reached one finger toward her cheek…no…toward her lips.

Just in time, he remembered the cost of love.

He would never pay the price of losing his heart again.

Lilleth turned onto her back, lay her splayed hand on her chest…she smiled in a dream and he wondered if it was about him.

Resolutions, he feared, were much easier to make than to abide by.

With effort, he pushed up from the mattress, backed across the rug and then went out of her chamber.

Safely on the other side, he leaned against the door and

groaned. One day soon he was going to have to face the challenge of getting an heir without handing over his heart in the process.

He was glad it was not happening tonight. Tonight, there was a good chance that he would have lost the battle.

A restful sleep was what he needed in order to gather his senses…to become the reliable provider that Aberly required him to be.

Lilleth was not certain why she awoke this morning feeling cheery as a lark. She had fallen into bed exhausted and slept soundly through the night even though she typically had trouble sleeping well in a new bed.

But somewhere in a dream she had felt a presence. It made her smile, gave her comfort.

She raised her arms over her head, stretched to greet the morning.

As if the movement summoned her, the maid entered her room.

"Good morning, my lady. Here is your breakfast."

The woman's attitude was so sunny and pleasant, Lilleth did not have the heart to refuse the tray.

"I will return to dress you in an hour." With a nod she left the room.

Lilleth couldn't say she'd ever eaten breakfast sitting in bed, nor had she been dressed by someone else, not since she was small and her mother did it.

There were some odd customs that came with being a lady.

Too odd to get used to all at once. She wriggled out from under the tray without spilling anything, then carried her breakfast to the chair in the bay of the window.

Sometime overnight the storm had blown out leaving

bright sunshine behind. Down below in the garden a breeze was blowing, twisting golden leaves which were still glistening with raindrops. She imagined, though, it was colder outside than it seemed.

She ate a bite of toast and jam, chewing quickly. The cocoa was hot, but she blew on it and drank it in quick sips.

If she hurried, she'd dress herself before the maid returned.

The plan for the day was to take a walk in Central Park to mark the first public outing as Viscount and Viscountess.

Was her new life to be all about ceremony and being seen doing certain things? She caught the little shiver tingling down her spine, looked ahead at the new road she was walking.

She meant to be a success as Viscountess and make River proud he'd married her. At the same time, she meant to remain who she was.

Which was a woman capable of dressing herself.

The gown she was to wear was already hanging on a hook so she did not need to decide what sort of dress suited a viscountess taking her morning exercise.

There were many new customs she would need to accept, as senseless as they might seem to her, but not this one of having someone else dress her.

Halfway into the undergarments, she was struggling.

"What is wrong with my old ones?" She tugged the corset. Luckily it laced up the front so after only a short battle with the frilly beast, she stood victorious in front of her dressing mirror.

The green-striped gown went on easily, but she did mutter something unpleasant to the dainty walking shoes she was forcing her feet into.

But then once they were laced up… "Oh…but you are lovely."

She lifted her skirt posing thc shoes this way and that.

"We might get along just fine."

Having beat the return of the maid, she went to stand beside the window. The view was nearly the same as the one from her old room, and yet everything looked different.

Especially the man walking through the garden. Judging by the way he was dressed, he was coming from the stable.

To her eyes River was a different fellow than he'd been yesterday morning. It must be because he was now her husband and it made all the difference in how she viewed him.

Before, she'd admired his long manly strides, but did not allow her thoughts to take her imagination much further than that.

Not so this morning. River Halston was now her husband and she enjoyed wondering what those long legs would look like without expensive trousers covering them.

She pressed her nose to the cool glass, sighed. If she was to discover intimate details of his person, it meant he would have to visit her chamber.

Something he had not done last night. She would have sensed his presence if he had. She would have roused at once and invited him to stay. No…*beguiled* him into it. The idea seemed intriguing, except that she had little notion how to beguile.

When Lilleth was younger, her mother used to worry that she was too curious about matters of procreation, but it was what came of being raised on a ranch. Nothing was out of the sight of a curious child.

Her parents had turned her head when the mares and the stallions took an interest in one another, but she'd peeked anyway. Now it was time to know what it was all about when it came to humans.

How hearts could connect and bond by an act that was of the flesh was an intriguing mystery. And how, the wonder of all wonders a baby could result…a child to love for all time.

Watching River stride across the garden, she anticipated the coming night. Surely, he intended on visiting this evening.

"But why didn't you come last night?" she whispered, her breath fogging the glass.

She had a guess why, of course. She did not yet have enough of his heart for him to dance that particular fling with her.

Wasn't a wedding night meant to do that very thing? Bond hearts and establish a family?

She truly was fond of her new husband and given the way he'd kissed her, she'd assumed he was fond of her, too.

And yet she'd spent the night alone.

The bedroom door opened. "Oh, my lady! You've dressed yourself…well never mind, let me just see to your hair, then."

Lilleth perched dutifully on the stool watching in the mirror while she was transformed.

Lilleth Younger faded away; Lady Aberly came forth.

River had just shrugged into his coat when there was a soft tap at his chamber door. Before he gave permission to enter, Lilleth came in.

He was not used to anyone entering without permission, but he was not used to having a wife, either.

Ah, but she was a vision in green and cream stripes

wearing a modest hat having a single bow with ribbons trailing down her back.

It was difficult to mind the intrusion.

"I see you are ready for your first foray into Society as Lady Aberly."

"Perhaps I am. We will soon see."

"Are you nervous?" There was a hint of it in her smile. "No need to be. You look fetching this morning."

She twirled once about. Her skirt caught a beam of sunlight streaming in through the window. It shimmered.

"Thank you, husband."

Hearing the title spoken so sweetly gave his heart a jolt. Joy or fear? He was uncertain.

"There is something I wish to—" she took a deep breath, let it out in a rush "—to speak with you about."

"Shall we sit?" It did not escape his notice that she slid a quick glance at the bed before she sat down in one of the chairs near the window.

He sat in the chair across from her. "What is it, Lilleth? Are you well?"

"Quite healthy. I just…well, I wonder why didn't you visit my bedroom last night?"

He should have expected such a conversation.

Maybe he should tell her that he had done so. That he had sat on the bed watching her. He did not dare do that, though. If he used the excuse that he'd found her sleeping she would expect him to come tonight when she was awake…in her bed and wearing who knew what sort of seductive gown.

"I meant to spare you," he made up. "We really do not know one another all that well. I would never presume to press my attentions upon you."

A long silent moment stretched between them. What was going on behind those lovely blue eyes?

"It had been a very long day and I assumed we both would want our rest," he added.

Not that he'd gotten much of it after leaving her room.

"Yes, of course you are right. Shall we be on our walk?"

With that, the matter seemed to be settled.

But it wasn't settled! At some point he was going to have to speak with her, make her understand how he felt on the matter of intimacy.

How could he though when he did not fully understand it himself?

Life would be a great deal easier if his bride had turned out to be the cold woman he had hoped for, wanting nothing to do with him beyond begetting an heir.

A lady who did not threaten to unbalance his heart and disrupt the way he needed his life to go.

Those were complications he must deal with at some point. For now he would simply take a walk with his wife.

Passing through the hotel lobby Lilleth pulled River to a stop in front of a new ice statue, which was identical to the previous one.

"Do you know this was brought in especially to impress you? All these flowers were, too."

"Were they? How do you know?"

She was not likely to forget the husband-coveting hussies she'd met in this very spot. "A couple of women said so."

"Why are you frowning? It's a beautiful sculpture."

"Lovely in every way…but those women were not. They spoke quite openly about how they wanted to seduce you away from me."

He lifted her chin, looked steadily into her eyes. "Let them prattle. I am not the sort of man to be unfaithful."

A question came to her quite suddenly…was there a

woman in his past whom he had left behind when he wed Lilleth's fortune?

Perhaps he had not come to her last night because there was someone he felt he was being faithful to.

The idea was too troubling to consider so she put it away in favor of enjoying the walk and her groom's company.

River had not strolled the length of the block with his bride before she clutched his arm and drew him to a stop.

"It's him!"

Alarm shot though him at Lilleth's anxious expression. "Snell?"

He drew her tight against his side, not convinced the men who wished to kidnap her would give up on the plot simply because she had married. Collecting a ransom might suit them as well as a forced marriage. Wicked men cared little how they came by money, only that they did not work to earn it.

"No, it's the little boy who sells papers. Look at him… he does not look well. We must help him."

Wriggling out from under his arm, she dashed after the child.

He hurried after her as discreetly as possible.

The young boy must have become alarmed seeing Lilleth's approach. He ran away with his newspapers littering the sidewalk behind him.

Even gowned in restrictive clothing, Lilleth was quick. River snagged her arm and drew her to a stop.

The dark alleyways in which the boy would probably seek shelter would be dangerous, especially for a lady dressed as affluently as his wife was.

"We have to find him," she pleaded. "You saw how he looked."

He lowered his mouth to her ear as if he were whispering loving words. Wouldn't people just love to talk about how the newlyweds were having a row on their first full day of marriage?

"We will, but not like this." She leaned away from his grip, he drew her tighter.

"If we wish to find him, we cannot go dressed like this. It will draw the attention of the worst sort of people. Come with me."

"Oh… I didn't think."

With a quick nod she followed him back to the hotel where she changed into the dress she had been wearing the first time he met her. He wore what he did when visiting the stables, but as disguises went it was a poor one. He would need something better.

Avoiding the elevator, he rushed Lilleth down the back set of stairs then across the garden toward the stables.

Along the way he plucked pins from her laboriously styled hair.

"Wait." He drew her to a stop then placed the pins in his pocket. He touched her hair, ruffling the stiff locks until they tumbled down about her shoulders. "It looked all wrong with your dress. Undone is less likely to draw attention."

"Why are we going to the stable?" she asked. "We will lose his trail if we don't hurry."

"This won't take long. I need to borrow a coat from the stableman. We'll take Morgan with us, too."

"Won't it be faster if we just follow the trail of papers before they blow away?"

"Living the way he does, the boy is skittish. He's probably not had reason to trust an adult. I've seen it before in London. Children are often exploited, used for profit but left on their own to survive. I'm hoping that offering a ride on Morgan will tempt him to come to us."

"It's not like this in Devotion Springs."

"It should not be like this here, either."

After a quick exchange with the groom, River snatched a ragged jacket from a peg on the wall and shrugged into it.

Within moments he and his bride were back on the street leading the horse and following the newspaper trail which had, unfortunately, blown in all directions.

They might, or might not be, going the right way.

But Lilleth had been correct about the child looking ill, the poor lad must be located at once.

"Slouch a little, River. You walk like a nobleman."

Which he was, of course. This man she'd married was noble and brave and wonderful.

Currently, she was relieved about the brave part of his character. She'd never seen anything like the part of town they were walking through.

It was dirty and vibrated with a shiver of foreboding. She felt eyes upon them at every corner they turned. Menace peered out of the shadows in a way she had never experienced, not even with the Snells.

She shivered all the way to her boots seeing the sorts of women standing in doorways and on street corners. And just as awful, the sorts of men seeking their favors.

"I wish I'd brought my rifle along," she whispered while walking close as glue to her husband.

"That would have drawn undue attention." He patted the pocket of the worn, humble coat. "I would not bring you here without protection."

"Look over there." Not wishing to draw attention to the spot by pointing, Lilleth tipped her chin toward an alley where a doorway was half hidden under a flight of stairs. “A child just went inside carrying a stack of newspapers. A little girl, I think.”

Please oh, please let something happen to change the child’s life before she ended up like the women in the doorways.

*Dear Lord...*she silently prayed that the “something” would be her, her and River together.

“Let’s go,” he whispered, gripping the horse’s reins. “Stay next to me and laugh...act like I just told you something funny. There are children watching us through the door slats. Laughter might put them at ease.”

“I think I see four of them...we cannot leave even one behind.”

“We won’t...just laugh. Then when we stop in front of the door make eye contact with one of them. Say something about riding Morgan.”

Lilleth did laugh, but it was hard. What had happened to leave these little children to live on their own, as seemed to be the case.

So far, River’s plan seemed to be working. The children had not scurried away from the door but peered through the wide slats in amazement at seeing the beautiful horse.

“It’s just a shame,” Lilleth declared, making sure her voice still held a hint of laughter. “Poor Princess here is as sad as can be. She sure does want a child to ride her.”

The name Princess suited the small horse and sounded friendlier than Morgan.

“I wonder where we would find a child who would want to ride her, though?” River patted Morgan’s white blaze. “If Princess could cry, I suppose she would.”

With the air turning colder by the moment and the wind

rising, they simply must get these little ones away from here…oh, and pray let the sick little boy be among them.

The door hinge squeaked. A small dirty face peered out of the opening.

"I'd like to help, sir…if it will make the horse not to be sad."

"Princess will be grateful, lad," River assured him.

The child came out, glancing cautiously about as if he feared something. Well, he must, mustn't he? This was a wicked awful place and he was no more than six years old.

If Lilleth followed her instincts she'd turn and run. It would be easier confronting a bear than the villains she sensed lurking in the shadows of this ally.

Someone was profiting off these little ones and they would not be happy to see them being carried off.

"Go inside while I set this one on Morgan…come back out and tell me what we are facing. Do it quickly. I have a bad feeling about this." River's voice was urgent in a way she had never heard.

Lilleth went to the door, squatted down to look eye to eye with the children peering out at her.

"Why, hello, there. May I come in?"

The little girl nodded, "Yes, ma'am."

Slipping inside Lilleth took a chill. This room under the stairs was dank…frigid. There were a few smelly blankets scattered about but no proper mattress.

She took the child's hand. It felt bony and cool but at least she had a hold of her and no matter what happened, Lilleth was not going to let go.

"Are there only the four of you?"

"There's five. Jimmy is back there sick as a dog."

It was dark in the back of the room but she heard the child coughing.

"What is your name, sweetheart?"

"Maddy."

"Well, Maddy, would you like to take a ride on Princess?"

Maddy nodded, her dark matted hair falling over one eye.

Lilleth led the little girl out and while lifting her up on the horse behind the boy, she flashed three fingers at River and nodded toward the door.

"Gracious sakes, don't you two look important sitting so high on this noble steed?" she asked, distracting the children while River went inside.

He came out no more than a moment later with a boy hanging on to his pant leg. A smaller child clutched that boy's hand. River carried the sick child.

"It's him," she whispered, meaning the boy with the newspapers.

"Are there any others living with you here?" River asked the boy clinging to his clothing.

When the boy seemed reluctant to answer Lilleth added, "We wouldn't want anyone to miss a turn riding Princess."

"There's no more of us, ma'am," Maddy admitted. "Not anymore."

The door over the stairs opened suddenly, crashed against the wall. A disreputable-looking fellow stomped out onto the porch.

"Hey there!" His face went red with his bellow. "Get your own workers. These'ns are mine."

River lay the sick child in her arms then lifted the smallest boy and settled him on Morgan's back with the other two.

"Take them out of here. I'll be along."

She would have argued for him to come with them, but

a hard expression narrowed his eyes. He meant to confront the villain and no argument would change his mind.

"Would you like to lead Princess?" She extended the reins to the last child and he took them without hesitation.

"When I had a ma and pa we had a farm with horses."

Lilleth nearly wept when she spotted a tear dripping down his brave little face.

Walking quickly on and pressing Jimmy tight to her, she glanced back over her shoulder.

River was dashing up the stairs, taking the steps two at a time. He had his hand in the coat pocket where the weapon was concealed.

"Who wants to sing with me?" she asked, summoning a cheery tone.

Not waiting for a response, she launched into a tune. Hopefully it was loud enough that the little ones did not hear the shouting coming from the alley.

It was past sunset when River finally brought his wife up the back stairs of the hotel.

Opening the door to their rooms, he placed his hand at the small of her back to usher her inside. Then he pointed at the couch in front of the hearth where a welcome fire blazed.

"Let's sit down," he said.

Warmth was what they needed to restore their spirits after the day they'd just spent. And food.

As if sensing the need, Mr. Gordon hurried into the room.

"Shall I have dinner sent up, sir?"

"Yes, thank you. And please ask the maid to prepare a bath for Lady Aberly."

Once the butler went out of the room, he sat down beside his wife, lay his head against the back of the couch. He sighed and closed his eyes.

"I imagine I smell like a New York gutter," Lilleth said giving him a poke in the ribs with her elbow. "But you smell worse."

He turned his head, opened his eyes to see her grinning at him.

"But we saved the lives of five children today, River. I say it's worth the stink."

"Yes, well worth it." He returned her grin even though grinning went against good sense. There was time for caution later. For the moment, he wanted to relish the satisfaction of their victory.

"It made me heartsick seeing how difficult it was to get the children placed in a reliable facility. Some of those places looked half as bad as the room under the stairs. How many charities did we go to? I lost count."

"Seven," he answered.

Lilleth was not the only one to have been sick at heart. Children had a right to be protected and sheltered.

In the past he had donated money for the care of orphans. How easy it had been to direct his accountant to do so.

"I'm glad Doctor Brown was willing to look at them right away. I wonder how much longer Jimmy could have gone without being treated. Poor little twig of a fella, he was in a sorry state."

"They all were. It was good of the doctor to set his other patients aside to see them," he said. "From what I've heard, Doctor Brown is dedicated to the care of both the rich and the poor."

A man to be admired…to be copied.

"We'll sleep better knowing those five babies are safe, but there are so many others like them who will be cold and hungry tonight." Lilleth pressed her lips together, shook her head.

He had to look away. This was not an appropriate time to be remembering how those lips tasted, how they felt pressed against his.

No time was appropriate…not for him.

"As Viscountess you are in a position to help…although not in the same way as today," he told her.

Lilleth held him with a steady look. He wondered if she meant to argue.

Let her try—he would forbid her to put herself at risk the way they had done today.

Lilleth noticed the moment when kissing her crossed River's mind. Too bad the expression did not linger. Rather it was there and gone before she had a chance to savor it.

But no matter. Surely kisses would come freely once they became closer as husband and wife.

River picked up one of her dirty tumbled curls, lifted it to the top of her head as if he were trying to put it back in order. With a laugh, he let it fall. "You were brave today, but from now on your help must be of the financial sort."

"I just hope you gave that wicked man something to lose sleep over."

"Possibly. My message was threatening enough to give us time to get the children away. But he is accustomed to rough living. I've no doubt he will replace his workers quite soon."

"Big cities are strange places. Is London like New York?" she asked. "Outrageous riches on one block and wicked poverty on the next? I never imagined such a thing."

All of a sudden she longed for wide-open land and the fresh air that whipped across it.

"I need to do more," she murmured. "What if those were our children, River? Our precious sons and daughters? We need to do more."

All of a sudden he gave her an odd look.

Worried perhaps? In the moment she was too occupied with her own thoughts to dwell on his. Sudden frowns were not uncommon for him, after all.

"As I said, as Viscountess you have the wealth and the influence to help."

Which she had done in Devotion Springs, but the need here was different…the children's plight far more desperate.

On the day she said goodbye to the children at the orphanage back home Lilleth had every confidence that they would be adopted by loving families.

She did not have the same hope for the little children they had just managed to place.

Today her eyes had been opened in a shocking way.

She sat up straight all at once, energized by an idea that just struck her.

A brilliant idea!

She shoved away the hair straggling across her face to better judge what River's reaction would be.

"Oh, I do intend to help. And you must help me."

"With what, my dear?"

His dear? Her heart made a small leap and twirl hearing the endearment. She should not read too much into it since people used it all the time. And yet the words did indicate a certain bond.

She should not get her hopes up…but at the same time, it was difficult not to. An endearment was an endearment. Perhaps he meant to pay his first husbandly visit to her bedroom tonight.

"Lilleth?"

"Oh!" How had she wandered so far from her brilliant idea?

"We are going to open an orphanage of our own."

Chapter Nine

A short time later, River sat on the chair in his bedroom looking down at the dark garden and giving thought to what Lilleth had just told him they would be doing.

Indeed, had told him quite baldly.

Perhaps she did not understand that one did not tell a viscount what he would do. It was the viscount who made decisions about requests presented to him.

Apparently when it came to marriage this was not how his wife perceived it to be.

Lilleth, he was learning, was a lady who was sweetly determined to have her way.

This was not the first time she had insisted on having it. Particularly where a decision about the funds that had come with her in the marriage was involved.

She had been willing to give him her fortune and yet she did not seem at ease releasing it completely to his care. Hopefully in time she would trust him to do what was best with it.

What he must bear in mind was that she gave up a great deal when she wed him. If she did not treat him with the deference he was accustomed to, he would overlook it.

What a pompous thought, he realized before it even finished passing through his brain.

The truth was, he liked her easy way with him. The last thing he wished was for his family to treat him as if he wore a crown. Marriage vows had been recited. Lilleth Halston was family.

Within the privacy of his home, he was simply a man like any other.

A man sitting on his divan noticing how thin the wall was between his chamber and his bride's.

The sound of sloshing water whispered through it.

Along with splashing, River heard singing.

Lilleth's tune was light and hopeful.

Evidently, with her new cause of founding an orphanage, the stress of the day lifted off of her.

What was she thinking of while stroking away dirt from the ugly part of town?

But why must he think she was stroking? She might be rubbing crispy, efficiently with the cloth.

That was not how it sounded, though…luxuriating sounded more the thing.

Especially since once the splashing and the singing stopped, she sighed. The contentment in the sound seemed a continuation of the alluring melody.

All of a sudden all he could think of was children…not orphans, though. Rather the ones a man begot from an intimate relationship with his wife.

Lilleth probably assumed him to be the sort of man who wanted children…perhaps many of them.

Yes, there had been a time when he was that man, but no longer.

The family that he'd wished for, Alicia had begun with someone else.

It hurt to recall the awful day when, his heart still raw with grief, he'd come upon Alicia at a musical laughing and flirting with another man. Weeks later he'd been stunned to hear the news of their engagement.

While it was true that he had been the one to put her aside, it had been out of duty. He'd no choice in the matter. The fact that Alicia had skipped merrily into the arms of Hugh Johnston made him wonder if she had loved him at all, that he'd imagined all that had been between them.

The old hurt picked at his scar in a way it had not for some time. Why was that?

Not because he was confusing desire for Lilleth with what he'd felt for his first love. He would give his wife what he could of himself, but it would not be his heart.

Water sloshed indicating that his bride had risen from the tub.

For all that he did not intend to give away his love again, it was entirely too tempting to imagine how Lilleth must appear in the moment. Still damp...a towel draped around her. He did not need to imagine how sweet smelling she would be. The scent of violet soap seeped into his chamber from under the doorway.

What would his bride wear to bed? As forbidden thoughts went, it was as troubling as it was intriguing.

Sexual intimacy led to love. That was how matters of the heart worked. It was going to be a struggle to remain unmoved when it came time to produce an heir.

He turned off his lamp for the night. He needed sleep if he would be able to face tomorrow on a sure footing.

That was what he would have had done if Lilleth had not begun to hum.

All at once he felt like a sailor being lured by a siren's song.

He could not help walking toward the door dividing her chamber from his any more than he could help turning the knob.

* * *

After a well-needed soak in the tub Lilleth stood in front of the hearth naked, water dripping off her hair and her limbs.

The one small towel she held in her fingers would not be sufficient to dry all of her.

Hair it must be then. She wrapped her heavy strands in the towel, briskly rubbing. Once she finished she kept the towel on her head to absorb more water.

Hurrying across the room to her wardrobe she left foot-shaped puddles of water on the floor.

Goose bumps from the chill pebbled her skin. She opened a drawer then drew out a flannel gown which would both warm her and dry her.

What it would not do was look appealing if River decided to come to her tonight. She snatched up a gown of cotton that was so soft it was close to being sheer.

Holding one gown in each hand, she looked back and forth between them while weighing the advantages of each.

Flannel would be warm and help dry her off. The only advantage to the sheer gown was that it would look alluring if River paid his first husbandly visit tonight.

Well then, there was no choice at all. She shoved the flannel gown back into the drawer.

No sooner had she put the pretty sky-blue gown over her head than she heard the door between her room and River's opening. Given how wet she was the fabric clung to her, resisting every effort to draw it down.

She had barely got it tugged down her hips when she glanced up to see her groom standing still as stone in the center of the room. The most animated thing about him was the color of his robe. Red plaid had never looked so manly, she decided.

"Howdy, River," she said while trying to tug the damp fabric away from her chest. For all her effort, moisture hugged it to her in an immodest display.

Then again, what did it matter? Her husband had not come to her so that they could enjoy the pleasure of gazing at one another's sleepwear.

"I see that I have come at an inconvenient moment."

Or a perfect one as she saw it. Except that he was backing slowly toward his bedroom.

"Why are you here?" she asked because if not for the expected reason, why was he?

"It was a mistake," he mumbled.

If he meant that, he would not be gazing at her with lust. Virgin that she was, even she knew what was on his mind.

She plucked the towel from her head, shook her hair in a way she hoped would be seductive.

It might have been had she not rubbed it into one long tangle while trying to dry it.

Drat. She did not want him to go yet even if he had not come to properly make her his wife.

Since her semi-exposed womanly assets had not persuaded him to remain she said, "Will you hand me my robe, please. It's over there on the bed."

Striding across the room he snatched it up then brought it to her.

There must be something about the rug that was more fascinating than she was because he kept his gaze affixed to it.

Maybe it was because she was wearing so little and so was he, but when his fingers touched hers when he handed her the robe…well, she yearned for those fingers to cover her hand, her arm and then…

But they did not.

When he pivoted about seeming as if he could not escape her quickly enough, she clasped his hand and held tight.

"Why did you marry me?" she asked.

He did look at her then, his brows arched in apparent puzzlement.

"We both know why."

"To a degree we do," she answered while slipping her arms into her robe. Luckily it was flannel, a pretty match to the gown she ought to have worn. She was done with being exposed and found wanting…done and a bit heart-sick. "I need to know more."

Perhaps if she did she would understand his reluctance to join her in the marriage bed.

"You sit over there on that chair." She pointed to the one nearest the door. "I will brush out my hair over here."

With the distance of the room between them she sat down and picked up her brush. Unfortunately she had done such a vigorous job with the towel it was a hopeless knot.

"What a miserable mess," she muttered then tossed the brush on her lap.

To her amazement, River uttered a quiet laugh.

"Here, let me do it." He carried his chair across the room and set it down behind her chair.

"Brush my hair?" She picked up the brush when he held out his hand for it. "I wouldn't think it among a viscount's skills."

"It is when he has three nieces and their nanny is back in England. Clara cannot be everywhere at all times."

He sat down. She made a mental wager with herself that he did not have the skills to conquer this mess.

His fingers plied her hair gently, separating the largest tangles. She'd never lost a mental wager so quickly.

"You have more patience than I do. I'd have had half my hair broken off by now."

She sighed, went soft inside. His fingers stroking through the strands felt a great deal different than when her maid did it.

"You know the reasons we wed, Lilleth."

He picked up the brush and drew it through the strands over and over again until they slid thought the bristles like water.

"I know why I wed you. You were really my only option and of course it was my father's last wish for me and Mama to join English Society. I know he approves even though he cannot tell me so." Although she no longer had a single snarl in her hair River continued to brush. "But you must have had a dozen ladies to choose from."

"Lilleth Younger, you are a curious woman."

"Lilleth Halston."

"Of course. A simple slip of the tongue," he said.

Yes, those kinds of things did happen…upon occasion. She only wished it had not been this occasion when all that separated them was his reluctance to…Never mind.

The situation was what it was. For now.

She turned about in her chair. Took the brush from his fingers. Even though she was now fully covered, the same feeling of longing to be touched crept up her arm when their fingers met.

"Honestly, Lilleth, you were my only option as well."

"Surely there were wealthy British ladies you might have wed."

"I do not wish for this to sound harsh because I am grateful that you agreed to be my wife…but the truth is, none of them were as rich as you. And as you are aware, Clara, Deborah and your mother all had their hearts set on us."

"Oh, I do know. All of them are over the moon. But, River, what happened to cause your family to be so close to ruin? I cannot imagine it had anything to do with your financial management."

All at once he gave his attention back to the rug, which to her eye was quite plain. Clearly it was something other than patterned wool that he was seeing.

"It happened slowly, over a period of years. My father let our finances go to ruin. I take some of the blame. I ought to have been paying closer attention. The issue was that he loved my mother to the exclusion of anything but their own pleasure. Later after my mother died, he further ignored his responsibilities by dallying with a long line of title seekers."

"It must have been difficult for you." She'd heard some of his story before they wed but certainly not all this.

There was something that she needed to ask. Any woman would wonder.

"River, didn't you wish to wed for love? Was there perhaps someone who—"

All at once he stood up.

"As I said, you are very curious."

"Given the circumstances of our marriage it is only natural for me to—"

"To wonder if I pledged wedding vows to you while in love with someone else? I did not."

Before she could ask who it was that he had not been in love with, he was gone, the door closed solidly between them.

But of course…a man like him…how could she expect he hadn't had former loves.

She twirled a strand of nice smooth hair in her fingers, smiling because there had not been an abandoned love… at least when they wed.

River's heart was hers and hers alone to win.

* * *

A week later River wished to show her a property which he believed would be perfect for their orphanage.

Sun shone down upon the open carriage while they rode the few blocks to view it. Brightness and the warmth did a great deal to rally Lilleth's spirits which had begun to sag.

So many days had gone by and still she felt no closer to winning her husband to her bed than she had before.

At least, though, she understood what might be keeping him from her. The example of his late father. River, being the responsible viscount that he was, feared making the previous viscount's mistake.

She glanced over at him, mentally shook her head.

Poor River was prone to presenting a glum attitude. To not counting his blessings which, to her way of seeing it, were many.

Where was the man Emily new? The one who had danced with her and sung to her?

Hiding from himself was where!

What she must do was lure him out by presenting a sunny frame of mind.

Surely that would win back the man she'd gotten a glimpse of?

"This is a perfect spot to suit our needs," he announced when the carriage halted in front of it.

At first sight, she decided it was not.

Giving him a sidelong glance, she feared that this endeavor would not form a bond between them, but a wedge.

"The area could not be better," he explained while helping her down from the carriage. "It's only a few blocks from the hotel. There will be no shortage of ladies offering their time for charity work."

"And that is admirable, but of little help to the children in the most desperate need," she pointed out.

"This is a safe area, Lilleth. There are even two other homes for needy children nearby."

"And that is the trouble. It is a safe area and the children who need our help are in dangerous areas." River's confident smile sagged. She spoke quickly before he could rally an argument. "How will they get here? How will they even know there is help available?"

"Surely you are not suggesting we shelter them in the slums they come from… I know you well enough to believe you will wish to go and settle the children even though we will hire a reliable staff. I will not have you putting yourself at risk."

"Children are falling ill, even as we stand here discussing the matter. We must find someplace else. I remember a vacant building near that ally where we rescued the children."

"No."

"What do you mean…no? That is narrow-minded of you to not consider—"

"I will give you your orphanage, but it will be here."

"It is not my orphanage, it is ours. And it cannot be located here. Again, how do you expect the children to make their way here? We would need to go and gather them up."

Which, when she considered it further, was a brilliant idea!

Tapping her lips in thought, mulling the matter over, up and down, side to side, she decided that this large home made a great deal of sense.

"What are you thinking?" her husband asked, sounding a bit uneasy.

"I am thinking you are correct. Let's purchase this one."

"Why the sudden change of mind?" Wrinkles creasing his brow indicated skepticism.

"Because you are a viscount. Everyone realizes they know best in all matters."

"Ah..." He took her chin between his fingers, lifted it and peered deeply into her yes. "But you do not believe that."

"This time I do."

"Why?" he asked without releasing his hold on her chin or her eyes.

Or her heart. It was beating in the quick, nervous way it did when she sensed he was thinking of kissing her.

Which he was probably not thinking of doing...but she was.

"It is only right that the employees we hire to run the orphanage should live in safety." She did her best to say so steadily but looking expectantly at his lips made her breathless. "Clearly the children will thrive among the flowers and the trees."

"A moment ago you dismissed the benefits of this location."

"That was before you promised we would go and gather up orphans."

"I made no such promise."

She patted his fingers, drew them away from her chin and then gave her attention to the window boxes.

Since the building was empty and the season turning, there were no flowers spilling prettily over the sides. It was easy to see how lovely they would be with a bit of nurture, though.

A vision of her own home filled her mind. Through the windows she spotted her future children laughing and running about.

Yes, one day it would be true.

"Not in words, you didn't. But surely it was your intent. How else will we fill our house…the orphanage I mean, with children?"

"Very well, Lilleth, I will hire a man to find children and bring them here."

While disappointed that he had not caught her reference to their own children, she gave him a bright smile.

All it needed was a bit of time and growing affection between them for River to share her dream of family.

She was as certain as could be about that.

In the meantime, they would work together to aid the helpless little ones of New York.

And of London, once they made the very long journey across the ocean. Once home was not here, but there.

It was the way of life, of course. Ladies married and left home every day.

Why, she was looking forward to the adventure of it, she reminded herself while spinning away from River so he did not see the gathering mist in her eyes.

River sat at the desk in his study watching steam rise from his teacup and thinking of the morning he'd spent with his solicitor, Mr. Levitt, instructing him on the purchase of the orphanage building and the hiring of a staff.

It was no surprise that Lilleth had insisted upon sitting beside him through the meeting, expressing an opinion on every order of business.

Evidently it was true, what she had told him about learning finances at her father's elbow. If anything, she had been modest in professing her ability with numbers. She knew how every dollar should, or should not be spent.

When she proposed that there should be ponies for the

children, both River and Levitt protested due to it being frivolous and expensive.

It took only a moment for her to win them over. Horses, she pointed out, would be a healing comfort to children who had been through too much misery in their young lives.

He found himself smiling on the inside when Lilleth pointed out to Levitt how this and that expense might be shifted to allow for the expense.

Earlier, at the start of the meeting, the solicitor had gently suggested that Lady Aberly might enjoy a more ladylike use of her time.

He'd thought of setting Mr. Levitt straight but decided to let him learn for himself what Lady Aberly would like to do with her time.

But ponies! He nearly chuckled but caught himself just in time.

A level head was what was called for, especially since even while he had been conducting business his wife tempted him to revert to the incautious man he used to be.

He had wished for a sober-minded woman who would demand nothing of his affections.

Instead he had gotten Lilleth. A woman whose hair he had caressed long after the tangles were gone. A woman whose sheer nightdress clung to her wet skin. The image was scored into his mind and no matter how many times he dismissed the vision, it came again.

In the future he would need to be more guarded when it came to her. If he was not, his wife would walk straight into his heart. Once she got in there it might be beyond his ability to get her out.

To his consternation he found himself continuing to dwell on a half-transparent blue nightgown.

What a relief it was to hear feminine voices chattering in the main room. A distraction was called for.

He rose from his desk and went into the main room.

It looked as if the shopping trip the ladies and been on was successful.

What had Lilleth purchased, he wondered. Not that he cared overmuch which pretty hats or gloves caught her eye. What he hoped to see was that the new viscountess found pleasure in spending the allowance she had scorned.

It was important for New York Society to see the Viscountess unconcerned about the financial stability of the viscountcy. A show of affluence was especially important given that he had been so close to being scandalously bankrupt. If anyone back home had begun to suspect it, seeing his wife spending so freely would cut off gossip before it came out of their mouths.

Perhaps it would, at any rate. The fact remained that he had married an American Dollar Princess. There was sure to be speculation.

Lilleth's mother cheerfully ushered in three men, their arms laden with packages.

"Howdy, River!" Lilleth sent him the smile that knocked ever more insistently at his locked heart.

"I see you've had a successful shopping trip."

Two more men entered, equally as laden.

Shopkeepers would be counting their financial blessings tonight.

"Oh, River! Wait until you see what Mama and I managed to find."

Whatever it was turned her cheeks pink with pleasure.

The deliverymen set the packages near the window.

When they went out of the room, Lilleth handed each of them a large tip for their service.

"Look at this!" Lilleth opened a package then withdrew a small coat, turning it this way and that. She opened another package and held up a pair of tiny boots for him to admire. "We have some of what we need for the children who come to us after the orphanage opens. And on the way back Mama and I paid a visit to the children we placed in the other residence. They are all thriving, even Jimmy."

"Isn't it wonderful?" Mrs. Younger asked.

"I am pleased to hear it." There were so many boxes on the couch that there was no place to sit.

Shopping for the orphanage's necessities was not quite what he had envisioned of his wife's shopping trip. He'd hired people to do that.

Ladies of the upper crust must see Lilleth frequenting luxurious shops. The wives of his potential business partners must notice that she freely spent money and report it to their husbands who would then feel it was safe to engage in business with him.

There was so much more to acquiring frivolities than Lilleth understood.

And yet…he did not feel disappointed in what she had purchased.

Day by day he was beginning to see the beautiful heart Lilleth had.

To see it and to fear it.

That sunshine smile drew his attention to her lips far too often. The thing to bear in mind was that a man did not kiss sunshine without getting burned.

Hadn't it happened once before? Although Alicia had been moonlight more than sunshine, he had been burned.

No more thoughts of burning kisses! His job was to work tirelessly to increase Aberly's newfound fortune. To put it before anything else.

A man should have amicable feelings toward his wife and he would not deny that he did. If only his skin did not get hot and his nerves itch whenever he thought of her still damp from her bath.

Viscountess Aberly might be a delicate-looking slip of a woman, but she frightened him.

In a battle of hearts, he feared she would win unless he remained wary.

While he would be kind and attentive to his wife's needs, he would give himself fully to the welfare of Aberly.

"The Lyceum is the first playhouse to be electrified," Clara said walking up the front steps of the theater, arm in arm with Lilleth. River and Mama came up the stairs right behind them. "I am simply over the moon to see it. You know, Mr. Thomas Edison himself did the installation."

The four of them had been invited to dinner at Mrs. Henry Wilcox's home and afterward, to share her box for this evening's play.

They had also been invited by Mrs. John Cleary and Mrs. Thomas Clark. Evidently, everyone wanted to be seen socializing with Lord and Lady Aberly.

Mrs. Wilcox had won the prize simply because her invitation had arrived hours before the others had.

What an odd thing it was to be sought after, not because of who she was, but what she was called. River, having dealt with the situation all his life, assured her that she would become accustomed to it.

Lilleth was not certain she would. Lady Aberly, she was discovering, was at once admired, envied and resented.

She had heard every sentiment whispered just while crossing the lobby.

"Isn't she lovely? I hear she is admirable in her charity work for orphans." Was the first comment she heard, and a lucky thing it was since the next comments were not as kind.

"There are several ladies of quality whom the Viscount might have chosen… I cannot imagine why he picked her…"

Had there been a woman of quality in his past? Given how the ladies tended to fawn over him, she thought it likely.

"For her money, why else?"

She wondered if River heard the woman's mean comments. She glanced over her shoulder at him to judge his expression.

He must have heard, otherwise why would he be frowning so severely at the woman? Too bad the busybody was so engrossed in spreading gossip that she did not notice.

No matter, really. The main thing was that Lilleth saw. River's protective reaction gave her a nice glow inside.

From behind came a voice speaking in a British accent.

"Can you imagine the audacity of Lord Aberly? Marrying this American when we have been waiting all our lives to wed a title. There are not enough of them to go around as it is. I hope she trips on the stairs." The ill wish carried up the steps. It was hard to imagine that the speaker did not intend to be overheard.

Mama gasped.

Glancing again over her shoulder Lilleth gave her mother a reassuring smile. "Do not take it to heart, Mama."

Then, casting the gossip a glance that was short on the graciousness required of her new position she added, "Such sentiments are to be expected."

Hopefully, her viscount understood that ladylike behavior of the sort she was required to exhibit was not something one learned overnight.

"My dear," River said, stepping up beside her and tucking her hand into the curve of his elbow. "Let me escort you up the steps so that you do not trip."

My dear? This was the second time he'd used the endearment and yet she was not convinced it was genuine. He may have used it to put the awful woman in her place.

A place which was not Viscountess.

But in case the endearment was sincere, she tucked it into her heart where it glowed warmly.

At the top of the steps, River bent to whisper in her ear, "I am sorry for that, Lilleth. I wish I could say it would be different when we get home to England, but it will not be, at least not for a while."

"Oh, I'll manage just fine." She smiled up at him to cover her growing unease.

He may have sensed her discomfort, for he squeezed her hand.

She squeezed back, taking his reassurance and grateful for the comfort he offered. Not only in the matter of the gossips, but because Mama and John were going home to Apple Valley Acres in two days. She was not certain how she would bear up without them.

For now, she put on her bravest face since it would help no one if she felt sorry for herself. Inside, though, behind that expression, she was close to tears.

"I have you and Clara, and those darling girls. Many women in my situation have less." Saying so made her feel better.

"Yes, my dear, you do have us."

Her heart went limp. This time she knew the words were not meant for anyone's ears but hers.

She stopped herself from saying that when their children came, she expected to be as content as she had ever been.

That was a conversation for another time. They had reached their seats. Now it was time to see and be seen, not speak and be overheard.

"I like you, River," she whispered. "People can say what they like…but I'm not sorry I married you. You are not a title to me."

After a short hesitation he answered, "I like you too, Lilleth."

And then he lifted her gloved hand and kissed her fingers.

It may have been for the benefit of curious theatergoers who cast them discreet and indiscreet glances, but it warmed her nonetheless.

Being scrutinized was something she would need to get used to. She thought it might not sting as much if only River continued to look at her the way he was doing now.

Electric lights illuminating the auditorium faded at the same time lights on the stage brightened.

Then the curtain drew open. This was a magical moment which caused everyone to gasp and applaud.

Everyone except for Lilleth.

For her the magical moment was in her viscount's smile. It shone from his eyes, lit up his handsome face better than Edison's invention ever could.

Chapter Ten

It was late when they returned from the play.

Everyone except for River had retired to their chambers.

As was his custom, he sat in a big chair beside the dying embers of the fire then lit the lamp and settled in for some light reading. It was a good way to relax and put the day away.

Within moments, he heard voices outside in the hallway.

What business could anyone have, lurking at his door this time of night?

It was unlikely that the men who meant Lilleth harm had followed her, but he could not discount the possibility. He was not going to feel at ease over the matter until he took his family back to England.

Which would not be at once. He had business matters to attend to in New York. The meeting scheduled for tomorrow promised to be especially lucrative.

Also, the ideal time for travel between here and England was still a few months away.

He was glad of the delay since to his way of thinking, financial opportunity in New York was greater than in London. This city was ripe for profitable business dealings. He did not intend to allow opportunities to languish.

To his great satisfaction he'd already managed to increase what Lilleth had brought into the marriage. Greatly increased.

Proof, he thought, that he was not like his father, that he could control his desire for amusement and make Aberly profitable.

Pushing up from the chair he padded barefoot across the floor, then bent and pressed his ear to the keyhole where voices could be more easily heard.

Or sniffles as it turned out to be.

"It is not a difficult journey home if you take the train, my darling." And yet his mother-in-law sniffled.

"Yes, but soon I will not be in New York. There will be an ocean between us." More sniffles, these ones quite called for, he thought. "I'm going to miss you so much, Mama."

"Sometimes I wonder if we could have made another choice." Mary Younger's voice trembled.

Another choice? A choice which did not involve Lilleth marrying him?

The thought gave him a queasy stomach. Where would his family be right now had Lilleth chosen another way?

Ruined was where…his nieces and sister-in-law in rags…and still he would be estranged from Alicia. Her family would never have considered a pauper for a husband, titled or not.

"But… Mama, I do not regret the marriage." A quiet sob made him wonder if she did, that those words were for her mother's benefit. "My husband is a good man. Even if he is lacking in cheer much of the time, we get along fine."

"I am certain he is a good man, darling…only, I wonder if he is the one who would have made you happiest."

Happiest? He was close to speaking up…pointing out that marriage at the highest levels of Society did not have a great deal to do with happiness.

"I am happy. I already love my new family. I do not regret having a part in securing their financial security. You know how dear those girls are, and so much fun. And I am already close to Clara. We are nearly like sisters."

This was very good. He did want his wife to be happy and not feel a stranger in the family. Clara and his nieces would give Lilleth what he could not.

"The thing to keep in mind is that Apple Valley Acres is now safe," Lilleth said.

The expensive horse ranch was probably safe, but jilted suitors were known for seeking revenge. Not that Lilleth had ever considered a Snell to be a suitor.

Revenge was a nasty bit of business, though. That family of miscreants would have a twisted vision of what was the truth.

Now that Apple Valley Acres belonged to him he would need to give some thought to what could be done to keep the ranch and its people forever beyond their reach.

"Now, then," Mary Younger said, her voice sounding steadier. "We will dry our eyes and look toward the future. Once the babies begin to come, we will see that all we did was meant to be."

"I suppose we are simply going through growing pains right now. You are right, children will make everything worthwhile…only, Mama… I do not know how to do it without you."

Please do not let them begin sniffling again, otherwise he would do so, too. Life could be hurtful at times and this was one of them.

"No matter the time of year our little ones arrive, I will come to you. It's a quicker journey on the modern ships they have now. Much shorter than when I made the crossing with your father…not that we minded. Oh, my dear, how I envy you this time…a new bride, a handsome groom and your whole lives before you."

Guilt twisted River's gut.

His wife was willing to give him everything and yet what was she getting in return? A husband who was not willing to give her the large family she clearly wanted.

And all because he did not dare to risk losing his heart during the intimacy required of begetting a child. In as much as it was within his control, there would be only the one…his required heir.

Hearing Lilleth's and her mother's hopes, made his heart fold over on itself.

What sort of person had he become?

Not one he was proud of, for a fact. His mental look in the mirror was bound to keep him restless through the night. Not that it would change anything.

When it came to matters between him and his wife, he would enjoy her company…because he could not do otherwise. He would provide for her and give her a life many ladies only dreamed of.

He would offer her everything…except for his love.

As was becoming her habit, Lilleth rose before the maid entered her room. She dressed herself and then sat in the chair waiting for the breakfast which would be served to her on a tray.

Not that she would be able to eat one small bite.

This morning she would say goodbye to her mother and John. Not forever, but still…

She shook her head determined not to weep. She and Mama had done so two nights ago and then put the tears away, replacing them with excitement for the future of the family.

There was the expected rap on her door, but it did not sound light and quick like her maid's did.

Before she could bid the person to enter the door swung open and River strode in, carrying her breakfast tray.

He set it on her lap. "Hurry and eat. The train leaves in two hours."

"The train to where?" she asked.

Forgetting that she was not hungry, she picked up a slice of toast slathered in strawberry jam.

Perhaps they were attending a social event taking place some distance away. She'd heard that Newport was the place where the rich gathered, but that was in the summer.

"Devotion Springs. I think it would be wise for me to see the farm if I am to be sharing the operation with Mr. Dalton."

"And with me," she put in to make sure he understood she would not be left out.

But… "You are taking me home?" she murmured through the jam and bread which seemed suddenly stuck in her mouth.

"I do not intend to leave you out of anything. And you may return home whenever you wish."

Did he mean that? It looked as if he did since he was smiling quite openly.

Thus far into their marriage she had not known him to lie.

She set the tray aside. Snatching a napkin, she rose suddenly, went up on her toes and kissed his cheek.

There was a good chance that she was feeling the first fluttery, heart-swelling indication that she was falling in love.

"Shall we go?" He must have just noticed he was smiling for his sober expression fell back into place.

No matter, she craved his smile, but she was beginning to love his frown as well.

"Um…yes…but just, here…"

Somehow, she had forgotten to use the napkin and River ended up with a smear of jam on his cheek. She wiped it away.

She could not say how it happened, but the cloth wiped away the frown and brought back his smile.

"Just wait until you see Apple Valley Acres, River," she said nearly dancing in excitement while they walked out of the room. "You will be happy you married me if for no other reason than to acquire it."

"I do not need the ranch to be grateful for that, Lilleth. But I am anxious to see it."

Grateful was not quite the same thing as happy. For now it would do.

She did want much more, but she was a patient person.

Besides, the way he was looking at her right now could be interpreted as happy.

For one thing he was smiling at her. For another there was the nicest warmth in his gaze.

And this, only seconds after she felt the first inkling of falling in love with him.

It must mean something. Perhaps their hearts had unknowingly reached toward each other.

It was possible that love was sending out tender shoots on both sides.

Time would tell…only, she hoped it was not much more time. It would be lonely business being the only one giving her heart.

First thing upon arriving at Apple Valley Acres, River toured the large white house on the hilltop. It was unlike any of his other properties but as beautiful.

After viewing the house, and then having lunch, he spent an hour in the stable with John.

River had been given a great gift of property in his marriage. Along with the gift came the responsibility of caring for it.

He'd always understood his obligation to his wife's estate, but now that he'd seen it, watched people working to make Apple Valley Acres a success… Now that he'd seen how Lilleth looked at it with such love, he felt even more need to protect this place.

Especially since the people living and working here still seemed on edge over their unsavory neighbors.

After the discussion with John Dalton, River had discovered that the Snells were as bad as Lilleth claimed them to be.

John was not convinced that the danger had been eliminated by Lilleth's marriage. Although the Snells could no longer get the property through her, the family was inventive when it came to crime. Kidnapping for ransom would not be beyond them, according to John. He did fear for Mary Younger's safety once Lilleth was in England.

Also according to John, Lilleth had not been taken in the past for only two reasons. One, she was an excellent horsewoman riding excellent horses. The other was that Homer Snell was not like the rest of the family. More than a few times the young man had alerted Lilleth to danger and done what he could to turn it aside. And he'd done so at risk to himself. Slade Snell would deal harshly with a son who was disloyal.

No wonder Lilleth spoke fondly of Homer.

One thing was for certain. That family could not be allowed to remain in the area.

The next day River summoned Mr. Levitt to the ranch

and had a productive meeting with him which, if all went well, would remove the threat the neighbors presented.

Within days, everything was in order and he was prepared to carry out his plan.

It was a simple one that he was certain would work.

While he would rather leave Lilleth at home, there was little chance that she would remain there once she saw him riding off by himself. She took great pride in showing him every inch of the horse ranch.

Besides, the Snell family needed to see for themselves that Lilleth was now his wife and under his protection. And not only Lilleth but everyone living and working here.

The afternoon turned out to be a fine one for a ride. It was hard to decide what he enjoyed more, gazing at pastureland which stretched in every direction, or watching his wife riding gracefully beside him.

Pampered-looking animals galloped freely across the land, their manes and tails flying. He understood why Lilleth had been willing to wed a stranger in order to protect the ranch.

While everything here was different than at his estate outside of London, the heart and soul of these two properties were alike enough to make him a bit homesick.

Without a doubt, Lilleth was going to feel the same thing when they reached England. Hopefully Aberly Estate would soothe the ache.

While he could not give Lilleth his heart, he would give her some peace of mind where Apple Valley Acres was concerned.

"How far away is the Snell ranch?" he asked.

"Not far enough. Less than an hour's ride west of here. Why?"

"We are going to pay them a visit."

"Have you lost your mind? Do not kick the hornet's nest, River. Those are horrid, greedy men."

"Greedy is what I'm counting on."

"This isn't safe. Who knows what they will do."

He shot her a grin. "I've got a fair idea."

"Had I known that's where we were going I would have brought a rifle from the house."

He patted his coat pocket. "I would not leave you unprotected."

The fact was, he had two weapons. The one on paper would be the most powerful. It was certain to lay a greedy man flat.

"One viscount with a small gun against three remorseless villains," Lilleth gave him a narrow eye. "I have to say, River, I am not comfortable with our odds."

Not a bit comfortable.

Which for some reason made her husband grin.

For all that she was happy to see the rare gesture, this was an unlikely time for it.

"I have a better weapon," he told her.

"I hope you are not counting it being your title."

River was a man used to getting his way, to having people eager to do as he wished. All it would get from the Snells was a sneer.

Slade respected no one.

Too soon for comfort, they reached the property line.

"Are you looking for trouble, River? It is what you will get if we do not turn around."

"I would not put you in danger. But if you wish to wait here—"

"Alone! No, thank you very much."

Only a half a mile onto the property Lilleth spotted a rider coming fast at them.

River reached for his pocket.

"If you believe we are so safe, why are you going for the weapon?"

"Just in case I'm wrong." River urged his mount forward, riding ahead of her.

"You may put it away. It's only Homer."

The sun was low on the horizon making a dim silhouette of her friend who was waving his hat in probable warning.

Dirt clods scattered when Homer drew his horse up only feet from them.

"What are you doing here?" Homer glanced back and forth between her and River.

"I have come to speak with your father," River stated.

"You're the lord fellow Lills married, I reckon."

"This is my husband, River Halston."

"It is a pleasure to meet you, young man."

"Pleasure to meet you too, sir. But I reckon Pa's not going to feel the same way. Better get going while you can."

"Too late for that." River pointed toward a cloud of rising dust. "I imagine that is your family coming over the rise?"

"Great Caesar rising! Pretend I captured you."

Homer grabbed Lilleth's arm, but gently. "Sorry, Lills."

River speared him with a hard stare. "Let go of her."

"Yes, sir. But—"

Before Homer could speak further they were surrounded by hooting Snells.

"Good afternoon, Mr. Snell." River declared, the authority of his station clear to see. "Is this boy your son?"

Slade Snell gave Lilleth a hateful stare. He turned one even uglier on River.

"Wish he weren't, but he is."

"My wife and I came to pay a friendly call, but your son prevented us."

Her husband certainly was composed…and gallant.

"That a fancy way of saying he caught you trespassing?"

"If you wish to see it that way. I prefer to call it a social call…a chance for neighbors to have a conversation."

"A conversation…?" Slade's voice curled in a snarl.

Lilleth had always feared the cold look in his eye that indicated he would just as soon shoot a person as speak with them.

"What's to keep me from stringing you up and taking this girl for my son."

"The law, for one thing. Me for another."

Homer inched his horse closer to her, partly blocking her from his father's view.

Slade, Coulder and Adam began to circle them, snickering and laughing without humor.

"I have something to say to you concerning your threats against my wife. They will end today."

Hooting and jeers stopped. All three sons gaped at their father, probably expecting him to draw his weapon.

What only she could see, and perhaps River, was that Homer discreetly slid his hand toward his holster.

"Well now, I can't see any reason why they should."

"Let me make the reason clear to you. The Viscountess is my wife and under my protection. So is her family and everyone who belongs to my ranch. You will no longer harass them."

"Is that a fact? I suppose I should make it clear to you that you best be on your way before you are sorry you aren't."

"In time. Right now I have another matter to discuss with you."

Oh dear, what else could there be? River had already threatened bullies, waved a red cape at a bull.

Slade leaned forward in his saddle, giving deeper menace to his scowl. “Get off my property.”

“It’s the property I’ve come to discuss. I have a proposal to make.”

If River was intimidated by the growl rumbling in the elder Snell’s throat, it did not show. Her husband smiled cordially as if they were sitting politely across a polished desk from one another.

“You have a fine piece of property.”

Run-down from lack of care was what it really was, but Lilleth refrained from pointing out the truth.

“I sense you are a shrewd business man, Mr. Snell.”

What was her husband up to?

The man’s chest puffed up at the false compliment.

“I ain’t sellin’. This here land is for my boys in perpetuity.” He put great emphasis on the last word.

“Nor should you. As I said, it is prime property.”

Lilleth made a supreme effort not to roll her eyes.

“The issue is, I am not comfortable with you living close to my ranch. I have come prepared to make you an offer.”

“And I’m prepared to refuse it. This is where I raised my boys and buried my wives.”

“Hear him out, Pa,” Coulder said.

“Yeah, Pa. Maybe there’s money in it. We could move to Texas and live like kings if there is,” Adam said.

Slade Snell scratched his beard. Something that looked like a piece of dried weed fell out of it. “Don’t know what trickery you have in mind but my fool boys want to hear it.”

“It is not trickery, sir. I’ve had my lawyer look into the public records regarding this property and he discovered that you are behind on the taxes.”

"Wouldn't be if it weren't for you getting her first." Slade shot Lilleth a sneer that made her scalp prickle.

"If you disrespect Viscountess Aberly again we will ride away and you will lose this property."

"I want to hear what he's got to say," Coulder declared giving Lilleth a polite tip of his hat. "I regret the mischief I planned to cause you, Lady Aberly."

She did not think he did, but he was holding out something of an olive branch.

"Go on then," Slade grumbled.

"My lawyer discovered that you have done something unusual in regard to the deed of the property. You have listed yourself and all your sons as owners."

"Makes it harder for scalawags to try and steal it from us." Slade narrowed an eye at River.

"I have not come to steal from you, Mr. Snell. I only wish for you and your sons to move someplace else. To that end, I have had my lawyer draw up quit claim papers for you and each of your sons…with the exception of Homer."

"What's that? Sounds like some sort of trap." Slade gave River a narrow eye.

"No trick. Only a document saying that you release your interest in this property. There is one for each of you. In exchange for your signatures you will each receive a generous sum of money for you to begin life somewhere else."

"Texas, here I come," Adam said. "I'll sign it."

"What about Homer? You left him out of the signing," Slade said.

"Your son's name will be the only one remaining on the deed and the land will belong solely to him."

"I'll sign my name." Coulder grinned at his brother. "I hear tell there are lively saloons in Texas."

"You ungrateful whelps." Slade turned a hard eye on his children.

"I would say they are making a sound business decision," River pointed out. "How much money will you and Homer really make off the ranch, Mr. Snell? Less than what you will have by releasing interest in it…and it cannot be long before you lose it to the tax debt."

"Only the two of us here all on our lonesome. Won't be much profit in it." Once again he scratched his scruffy beard as if deep in thought.

"Reckon I'll sign your paper, then, since the land stays in my bloodline."

River reached into his saddle pack and withdrew some official-looking papers.

"Read them over tonight. I'll have my lawyer come by tomorrow at noon for your signatures."

"And he'll bring our money?"

"Of course." River nodded at them, one at a time. "You have all made a sound financial decision. I am certain you will not regret it."

River extended his hand. Slade simply stared at it. Coulder and Adam pressed their horses forward then shook his hand.

Giving Lilleth a nod, he said, "Let us be on our way, Lady Aberly."

He waited for her to turn her horse, then he followed close behind her for a short distance.

All she could do was look back and stare at him, marvel at his composure, his aura of authority.

No one had ever convinced that family to do anything.

"Tomorrow I'm headed for Texas!" Coulder Snell shouted.

Adam, yeehawed.

"Looks like we struck it rich after all, boys," the elder Snell brayed.

River urged his horse forward so that they rode side by side.

Lilleth glanced back again at Homer sitting astride his horse watching them ride away.

"I cannot believe what you just did. For all of us…and for Homer. You freed him from his family and made him a landowner. River Halston… I could just kiss you."

She'd meant it only as a teasing expression of gratitude, but once the words were out she realized how much she truly wanted to.

Watching River's lips go tight at her comment told her it would not happen.

"There is something I want you to understand," he said.

Her breath caught. Something about kissing him? Please let him be thinking of it too even if he did not look like he was.

"I am not using your money to buy off the Snells. I recently made a profitable business deal. I want you to know that."

"I would not have minded if you did. So long as they are gone."

"I would have minded, though. You are my family now, Lilleth. It is for me to protect you and I will do it out of the funds I earn."

River Halston was her hero, her knight in shining armor. Just this moment, she fell a little bit more in love with him.

The sun had set by the time Lilleth and River came within sight of home. The moon hovered over the horizon big and bright giving enough light for her to show her husband one more special place.

"Come with me." She turned her horse, urged her to a trot.

It did not take long to reach the family cemetery.

All the way home Lilleth had been thinking about the amazing thing her husband had just done. She had never known anyone like this viscount she had married…had never felt for anyone what she felt for him. More and more her heart was reaching for his.

"Here we are." Dismounting her horse she tied its reins to a fence post.

Some people might find this a place to be fearful of in the moonlight. Lilleth found it quiet and comforting.

"This is the family plot," she explained while River secured his horse next to hers.

"There is one like it at Aberly's country estate. I've never visited at night, though."

"No? I find it to be a perfect time. Everything is so restful— memories come easier." She bent to touch her brother's small headstone. It appeared pearly in the moon's glow. "Sometimes I imagine I hear their voices even though they died before I was born. Will you sit with me on the bench?"

There were three of them but she picked the one closest to her brothers.

"I want to thank you for what you just did, River. There are no words to say how grateful I am. You took a great risk." And now because of him she was safe in a way she had not been in a long time. "You were very brave."

"Not really. I knew what they wanted, my dear."

Was she his dear? He'd called her that before. It made her glow inside thinking it might be true.

"Nevertheless, I'm glad you brought along the gun."

"A man cannot be too careful and I would never risk your safety."

"And I appreciate that, but I wonder…being a gentleman, how is your aim? Can you shoot a can off a post?"

He laughed. The wonderful sound shot through her heart, rather as if it was that can on the post.

"You don't know this about me, but I'm an excellent marksman. I take first place in competition every time."

"I shall sleep secure at night knowing it," she teased, nudging him in the ribs with her elbow.

He nudged her back, grinning.

In the moment, it felt like they were River and Emily again.

Night closed in, wrapping them in a blanket of cricket song and whispering grass.

"They…" She pointed her finger at her brothers' small headstones. "They were only two and three years old when they died. I missed having siblings so much. You are lucky to have had a brother. Will you tell me about him?"

For the longest moment he simply stared down at her brothers' graves so she thought he would not answer.

"My brother's name was Harold. We were close growing up…each other's best friend…worst foe sometimes, too. And, yes, I was lucky to have him."

"How I envy that. I would give anything to have grown up with my brothers. Our adventures would have been splendid."

"I'm truly sorry you did not." She felt a kiss lightly brush the top of her head. She went fuzzy for an instant, except for her lips. They went tingly. "Influenza took Harold when he was twenty-four…a young husband and father. Days before, it took our father. Nearly Clara and the girls, too."

"I cannot imagine how awful it must have been for you. To face that alone…"

He looked as if he would respond, but then did not.

"Well, you are not alone any longer. You have me."

Still, he remained quiet. But then he touched her chin, lifted it, peered into her eyes.

"I do, indeed." He kissed her, so quick and light it could have been the breeze.

Feeling emboldened by the moment, she kissed him back, pressing against him and giving part of herself with it.

"Lilleth, I…" Hands on her shoulders, he gently pushed her away. The openness that had been in his eyes a second ago vanished. "We ought to get back. Did I hear something about bears and bobcats in these woods?"

No one had ever confused her as this man did. Confiding his heart one moment then becoming suddenly distant? It made little sense.

"River Halston, you just faced down the terrors of Devotion Springs. Why do you fear kissing me?"

There was one possible reason that she did not wish to consider, however if she was to understand his reluctance she must ask him again. "Is it because you are in love with someone else?"

"No, Lilleth. I am not. There was no one standing between us when we spoke our vows."

"I confess, I am glad to hear it." Why then would he not allow her, his wife, into his heart? "I imagine, though, there were more than a few ladies who vied for your affection."

"It's the price a man pays for being a viscount."

"But, River, it seems a sad thing to me. You are such a handsome man. So smart and brave. I cannot believe no woman has seen past your title and fallen in love with the man you are."

The moon must have become fascinating, for he stared fixedly at it…or, was it at a memory of his past?

"Who was she?" She touched his hand.

"Her name was Alicia."

"And you were you in love with her?"

"All the men were in love with her. She was very beautiful," he said, finally looking at her.

"But she loved you?"

"No. I will tell you the truth, Lilleth. When I knew I must wed for a fortune, I broke it off with her. Within three months she was wed to someone else and blissfully in love. So, I cannot say there was ever love between us."

Good then. It was a relief to know that there was not a woman he was pining for. It was going to be challenge enough to win this man's heart without another woman standing between.

"We should go to the house. People will be worried," he said, reaching down his hand. His fingers closed about hers with such a sensation of affection. She could not possibly be imagining it.

"I realize you do not love me, River…not now. I did not expect that you would right off. In a marriage such as ours it is only reasonable for it to take time. But I confess that I am glad you are not in love with someone else."

She gave his hand a lingering squeeze since she assumed he would not appreciate her stealing another kiss.

When next they kissed, and she was certain they would, he would be the one to offer it…freely and with his heart.

"What does a bear growling sound like?" Her brave husband went tense. He curled his arm protectively around her shoulder.

"Not like that raccoon peeking out of the bush." She tugged him toward the horses, shaking her head and laughing under her breath. "Come, River, let's go home."

Chapter Eleven

Three days after his visit with the Snells, River walked out of his office escorting Mr. Levitt across the main drawing room of the suite. It was risky going with having to dodge three young girls and their toys that were scattered over the floor. Not to mention an energetic puppy dashing underfoot.

Levitt did not seem to mind. The solicitor was smiling as broadly as River was when he bid him goodbye.

River walked toward his study but had to catch his balance when the puppy dashed between his feet.

Before he reached the safety of his office, Lilleth came out of her chamber.

"Ah, the very person I was hoping to see." And not only because he had news to share, but because whenever she crossed his path, she smiled.

Of course, many people smiled when they saw him, but Lilleth's smile was something apart. It was sweet and genuine. It never failed to make him feel brighter inside.

"The Snells have gone. Mr. Levitt paid a visit to the ranch and was certain the only one remaining was young Homer."

"That is the best news!" Lilleth swept up the pup and spun him about. Her skirt flared about her ankles. He felt joy rippling from her and straight into him.

As much as he tried not to react to her happy influence, sometimes he simply could not. Crack by crack she was chipping away at the wall he'd built against her.

A useless wall. What good was it when she continually leaped over it?

"Thank you, for that." She folded River in a tight, one-armed hug.

His wife smelled like a flower, although he could not think of which one because she also smelled like a woman. The combination of the two was distracting…dangerous.

No matter the temptation, he would remain cool… friendly but not enamored.

So, he patted her on the back and set her at arm's length.

"River," she said, thrusting the wriggling pup at him. "We need to discuss what will become of Homer."

"Of course." He made sure to smile because his wife had done nothing to earn his distant attitude. It was not her fault that he could not give her what she wanted of him.

He set the puppy down. It caught his pant leg in its sharp little teeth and tugged.

"Shall we go someplace less risky?" she suggested.

His chamber perhaps? It might not be the place she had in mind, but the idea charged into his mind with no regard for caution.

"Over by the window should do," he said.

Outside the wind blew hard, leaves and small twigs hit the glass.

"What is it about your friend you wish to discuss?" he asked.

"Now that he has property, he must have a way to support it. I wish to offer him a job at Apple Valley Acres."

"We shall hire him, then."

He owed Lilleth far too much to refuse her that.

"I also wish to pay the taxes on the property. I owe Homer a great deal."

"We shall do that, too."

Just then his youngest niece climbed onto his lap and snuggled in.

"These rooms are rather small for all of us. There is not much privacy. Do you wish for me to rent us a house until we leave for London?"

"When, exactly will that be?"

"I still have quite a bit of business to attend to, so several weeks, I think."

"Would you mind if we stayed here? I like the coziness and for such a short time there is no reason to uproot everyone. Besides, the orphanage is only a few blocks away. It is convenient having it close by."

"Very well, we will stay here."

He was glad because he also liked the coziness of these rooms. Also, employing the staff which would be required for a new residence would be impractical for such a short time.

Many wives of Society would demand grand accommodations, elegance and expensive surroundings.

Lilleth was not a woman prone to vanity for which he was grateful.

It occurred to him that his elegant Alicia had been vain. How had he not noticed it before?

His niece crawled out of his lap and onto Lilleth's where she fell promptly asleep. Lilleth stroked the curls away from Violet's cheek, her smile full of affection.

As he recalled, Alicia rarely spared a glance for his nieces.

Lilleth was meant to be a mother.

He feared she would not be content with giving him only the heir he required.

Still, it was the way it must be.

He had no intention of giving his heart away in the marriage bed.

The only thing Lilleth enjoyed about having lunch at the home of Mrs. Julius Fairmont was spending time with Clara.

And, she supposed, the tiny iced cakes. They were delicious. She'd eaten two and might have reached for a third if she did not fear the judgmental glances of the other ladies.

What a long affair it had been…socializing before the meal, then the meal and now a stroll in the garden.

In all, the luncheon was approaching four hours. Her time would have been better spent at the orphanage, preparing it to welcome children. She must have everything in order so that it would run smoothly once she went to live in London.

Here she was ambling past rosebushes not in bloom, under trees with amber leaves dangling and listening to women chatter about fashion.

Did anyone really care what color Paris deemed a Christmas gown should be?

"Dressing seems to be a sport to them," she muttered to Clara. "Surely they have more important issues to speak of."

"No doubt they would if there were not certain topics considered unladylike to discuss. I fear we are limited to speaking of fashion, children and one another."

"I could speak of your children all day long, Clara."

Especially since it did not seem she would be speaking of her own anytime soon.

"So could I, but we are supposed to mingle and chat about nothing with the other guests. Shall we join our hostess over the by the fountain?"

Lilleth hoped this party would end soon. The wind was beginning to blow again and had a colder bite than it had this morning.

Reaching the fountain they found their hostess and four other ladies seated on a bench.

They were discussing two of the approved topics. Children and one another.

"Agatha Wilder is with child again, if you can believe it." A woman with a narrow face and a pointed nose said, her voice not at all discreet. "Apparently some among us do not know when to stop."

"Why, Merry Prentice…what a heartless thing to say," Clara put in. "I would have welcomed more babies if I'd had the chance."

"Naturally, I did not mean you. But Agatha had a child less than a year ago. Perhaps someone ought to speak with her about where babies come from."

The comment caused a titter from some of the guests.

"Given that this is her fifth," Mrs. Fairmont put in, "I rather think she suspects."

"When I have children," a lady with a British accent said. Baroness Smythe, Lilleth recalled her name to be. "I shall have the prescribed heir and spare. Then no more."

Heir and spare? Prescribed? Lilleth had not heard of such a thing.

"Surely you agree, Viscountess?" The narrow-faced woman asked. "Have the required child to keep the title going and then a spare one in case the unthinkable happens?"

What? A first child to be cherished and another to be a replacement…just in case?

How absurd. Did many people in River's world hold that opinion?

"I am certain I will be overjoyed at whatever children the Good Lord blesses me with," Lilleth answered coolly as she supposed her new position required her to…but an heir and a spare was one of the most heartless things she had ever heard of.

"As most of us are," Clara said, slipping her arm through Lilleth's. The clear message was that they were united in their view that each child was valued and cherished.

"It is a shame that my newest guest from London could not join us," Mrs. Fairmont said. "But she's just arrived and in need of a bit of a rest. I would be interested to hear what she has to say on the matter. She is expecting her first child, you know."

Happy exclamations tittered about.

Clara cast Lilleth a glance. "I must beg your indulgence, sister, but I am growing weary and do not wish to bring on a headache."

Then to their hostess, she said, "Won't you excuse us?"

Lilleth was not sure what pleased her more, being called sister or taking leave of the women who were probably about to gossip over the English guest's pregnancy.

How did they put up with one another?

Walking the path toward the house, Lilleth said, "I hope I am not a disappointment to your brother, but I wonder if I will be an acceptable viscountess. I will not be fond of this sort of entertaining."

Clara laughed. "Do not worry—I adore it. And it seems according to some that your highest duty to Society is to produce an heir and a spare."

As matters stood, she would produce no children at all.

"That is the worst thing I ever heard…calling a child a spare."

At a curve in the path, they nearly ran into a woman walking around the bend.

"Clara!" the highly fashionable lady declared.

"Why, hello, Alicia. What a surprise to see you here in America."

Alicia! Could she be River's Alicia…? Formerly his, of course.

"My husband has business to attend to here and I did not wish to be away from him."

The woman gave Lilleth a glance, clearly waiting to be introduced.

"Lilleth, this is Alicia Johnston…from London. Alicia this is Lilleth. I would adore to chat and get caught up but Mrs. Fairmont just mentioned how anxious she is for you to join them."

With that, Clara walked on, her fingers still clamped on to Lilleth's sleeve.

That was as brief an introduction as Lilleth ever had. Perhaps Clara was uncomfortable chatting with the lady who might have been her sister-in-law if life had gone differently.

There was certainly no need to be, though. From what Lilleth understood, Alicia had gone on to find happiness and River's heart had not been terribly broken over the split.

Maybe Clara did have a headache, after all.

Glancing backward at the lady, Lilleth thought River spoke the truth when he said she was beautiful.

Mrs. Johnston was elegant in every detail of dress. She carried herself as gracefully as a swan.

What River had told her was no doubt true. All the men were in love with her.

* * *

River escorted his wife and his sister-in-law, one lady on each arm, into the ballroom of the 5th Avenue mansion of Mrs. Gordon Crowley.

He'd attended her elegant event on a visit to New York two years ago. Mrs. Crowley always hosted in the fall so that there was no whisper of it being held too close to Mrs. Astor's annual ball held in January.

Clara seemed relaxed, and no wonder. She had been attending such parties all her life…and had hosted them many times.

Judging by the way Lilleth's fingers clamped his sleeve, she was nervous. Although she came from a prominent Connecticut family, she had spent her life in the country.

This ball, with the highest in Society showing off their splendor, must be overwhelming to her. And yet, she did not appear nervous, it was only the grip on his arm that gave her away.

Anyone standing in line to greet Mr. and Mrs. Crowley would believe Lilleth to be the soul of social grace… and beauty.

Especially beauty. Whenever he glanced sideways at her his heart thumped harder.

To deny he had been fortunate in the wife that circumstance dropped in his lap would be foolish.

Here was a lady who would be the viscountess to be dreamed of…socially graceful, kind and attentive to acts of charity. In all, a lovely ambassador for Aberly.

They had been here only a short time and he'd seen many gentlemen turn their heads when she passed by.

Lilleth's beauty was not like other women's. It was softer somehow…warmer.

When she smiled at a person it was with genuine pleasure to meet them. There was no calculation behind her gaze, no sense that she was gauging what might be gained by an association with them.

Lilleth was artless, sincere and beautifully candid.

Too many women in attendance adorned themselves with jewels in their hair…or even outrageous feathers. Their gowns were frosted in ribbons and lace.

His wife adorned herself with a smile. She wore small roses in her hair. A trail of pink and white buds began at her temple, drifted to the nape of her neck then peeped in and out of her curls.

She wore a silver gown that shimmered every time she took a step…or when she breathed. It was hard not to watch the threads sparkle when her ribs rose and fell.

Approaching their host and hostess, he glanced about making certain that he was the only man caught in the silver-threaded web encasing his wife's form.

As far as he could tell, it was her smile getting their attention.

"Howdy, Mr. Crowley. Howdy, Mrs. Crowley," Lilleth said, drawing River out of his flight of fancy and reminding him of the reason he was standing in this line.

"Good evening, Viscountess." Mr. Crowley took Lilleth's extended hand and bowed slightly over it.

A frizzle of annoyance at seeing their host touching his bride zipped over River's nerves. Which was silly given that this was a common, quite acceptable greeting. One which Mr. Crowley would perform a hundred times tonight.

It would not have bothered him in the least had the man's eyes not been glowing with a particular light…and had he not held her hand a second too long.

The man offered Clara the same greeting, but this time it did not make his nerves twitch. Perhaps because that twinkle in Crowley's eye had not been presented to his sister-in-law.

River returned Crowley's greeting more crisply than he ought to have. It was impossible that he was jealous. He knew what jealousy was. It had eaten him up after Alicia wed. He did not have the sort of affection for Lilleth to make him green-eyed.

She was, however, his wife which might account for the sense of possessiveness that came over him when the gentleman greeted her.

Coming into the ballroom, he scanned the crowd. He knew many of the men, having done business with them. He did not know the wives, though. It would be up to Lilleth, in her role of viscountess to make their acquaintance and secure connections which would benefit Aberly.

"There is Merry Prentice," Clara all but hissed. "We should walk in the other direction."

"What is wrong with Mrs. Prentice?" River asked. She looked pleasant enough to him and her husband had a fine head for business.

"Apparently, she dislikes babies," Lilleth whispered. "At least if there are more than two of them and they are girls."

Curse it. He did need to have a word with her about children. But it would be an uncomfortable conversation so he'd been putting it off.

He would put if off again tonight in favor of enjoying the evening.

"I am famished, sister," Clara said. "Come with me to the refreshment room."

Lilleth glanced up at him, "Will you come?"

"I'll join you in a moment. There are several gentlemen I must greet first."

He bent to kiss Lilleth's cheek.

As far as gestures went, there was nothing intimate in it. Indeed not, he also kissed Clara's cheek.

And yet…there was a great difference between the two.

Why had he done it?

To indicate to others that he was content in his convenient marriage? Or was it because he was more content in his marriage than he wanted to be and so had reacted to the urge to kiss her?

No more kisses, on cheeks or anyplace else, he silently vowed.

From here on out the only kisses he would give would be to his small, giggling nieces.

All Lilleth wished for was to browse the dessert table. It did not matter that she had yet to eat dinner.

Casual browsing was proving difficult to do. How was one to concentrate on pastries when her every move was being scrutinized.

She had been warned this would be the case, by Clara and by Mama. She was now a lady of high rank whom others would wish to emulate.

Lilleth joined Clara at the end of the long table. Together they sat in chairs which were hidden from view of the table by huge potted ferns.

"A moment's respite is just the thing," Clara commented.

While people could not easily see them, she and Clara had a nice view of the parade passing by.

So much elegance on display. What would Mama think of it all? This had been her life before she met Papa.

Clara had her fork raised halfway to her mouth, then set it on the plate with a clack when a tall, extremely elegant woman walked past on the other side of the ferns.

"Isn't that your friend Alicia from London?" She looked even more beautiful than she had in the garden the other day.

Since Clara had not introduced the lady as River's former interest, Lilleth did not mention it.

"I never said she was my friend, exactly. But will you excuse me for a moment?"

"Of course."

Lilleth had expected Clara to go after Alicia but she turned and went in another direction.

Luckily, Lilleth had a delicious little cake to give her attention to.

A pair, of rustling skirts came to a stop on the other side of the ferns.

She could not see who the ladies were, no more than they could see her.

"Lady Aberly is a bit of a mouse, if you ask me," one voice said.

Lilleth covered her mouth, stifling a giggle because she heard her mother's voice in her mind, warning her that she would be gossiped about and that she should not take it to heart.

And…compared to their flare and flash, she might well seem a mouse…dressed in a lovely silver gown, though.

"Not a feather in her hair or even a jewel."

"They say she is from the country and prefers horses to Society."

Nodding, she nibbled on the cake. What they said was true.

"I cannot see why the Viscount married her."

"She inherited a great deal of money and property from her father…it is the only explanation."

Also true, but the unflattering comment stung.

"I imagine there is no romance between them, given the circumstances."

Not yet perhaps! If she was not a lady who must behave above reproach, she would have thrown her cake at the gossips.

She sat as still as she could because it would be humiliating to be discovered overhearing this conversation.

"You do know what that means?"

What? Lilleth cocked her head to better hear what.

"The man is ripe for the taking. He will need a mistress."

No, he would not!

Lilleth stood up suddenly. The plate forgotten, it slipped off her lap but she caught it before it shattered on the floor.

All that was visible of the gossips were their heads and shoulders because the fern hid the rest of them. Because of her shorter height, all they probably saw of her were her eyes.

And theirs were about to be pierced right back with the righteous arrows of an incensed wife.

This time she would ignore her mother's advice not to speak whatever came into her mind.

At the same time, she must behave as a viscountess and not let her temper run wild.

Quickly, before the beet-faced women could get away, she came around the corner.

"Good evening, ladies."

Between them they could not produce a sound.

"Have you met my husband yet?"

Still silent, they shook their heads.

"No? It would be my delight to introduce you, then."

That brightened their expressions. Did they intend to apply for position of mistress on the spot?

Or, if they were as dense as fence posts, they might believe she had not heard that part.

Probably that, since she was behaving as if she had not.

"Ah, there he is," she said brightly even though her mood was dark. Perhaps she would succeed as Viscountess.

With a backward glance, she saw them grinning…and no doubt plotting. This was not the first time supposed ladies had spoken of stealing her husband.

River turned from a conversation he'd been having with Clara. Glancing around the room, he caught Lilleth's eye.

It took her aback to see his expression. Speaking with his sister-in-law had never made him look on edge before…

Wasn't it odd? Coming toward her he seemed to be gathering himself. He must have managed for suddenly, he smiled.

She nearly forgot her mission, but not quite.

"Lord Aberly." She called him that because it was what she was told was proper in a public setting. "May I have a moment of your time in the garden? These ladies are very anxious to make your acquaintance."

Luckily the garden doors were close at hand and the patio seemed to be deserted.

"Yes, of course." River's voice sounded odd.

"Are you well?" she whispered, certain the women did not hear because of their anxious chattering.

"Of course." He squeezed her hand. "Please introduce your friends, my dear."

At that, both women glanced his way…openly simpering.

"Oh, I do not know their names. But both of them wish to become your mistress."

"Is that so?" River bit his bottom lip.

What a handsome gesture. The home wreckers probably wanted him even more badly now.

"It is. They stated the fact quite boldly within my hearing and so I decided to bring them to you. To let you decide."

The young women seemed to be choking on their gasps, too stunned to run off, which would be wise of them to do.

"They are not the first to wish it, of course. But do you have room on your list for them?"

"Room…on my list?"

He shook his head, probably thinking she was the worst viscountess ever.

But she was a woman first…a married woman despite the fact that the bond had yet to be consummated.

His lips twitched. Would he laugh? This was a serious matter.

Yes, she had set a brilliant trap for the women and there was an underlying humor to it. But the situation was one which needed to be addressed.

"If you will give me your names, I will add you to the… the list. Although it is rather long," he told them shifting his gaze toward the dark silhouettes of garden shrubs.

Clearly River was trying not to laugh at them, but she would not mind if he did.

It was no more than they deserved for trying to ruin the family she had her sights set on beginning.

With matching gasps the women hurried away. Hopefully they had learned a lesson and would never again hope to seduce another woman's husband away from her.

Once they were gone, River bent at the waist, braced his hands on his thighs…and laughed.

Unrestrained merriment was not something she had seen from him before. It was reassuring to know he was capable of it.

"River Halston, laugh if you wish to and so will I." She poked him in the chest with her finger to make sure she had his undivided attention. "However, this matter of adultery is a serious one."

"Indeed it is."

"There will be no mistress for you, Lord Aberly. Whatever tawdry behavior you indulged in in the past, will end at once."

"Ah, Lilleth..." He kissed the top of her head then folded her in a hug. "You do know how to cheer a man. And just so you know, I have no tawdry past, nor do I believe in keeping a mistress."

"Good then," she muttered, snuggling her cheek against his satin vest. "Why did you need cheering?"

"It is nothing, really. Only, it is getting late and I am weary of performing my role as viscount. It can be tiresome after a long evening." He said this while staring at her lips. "Lilleth, I promise there is no list nor will there be one."

He gave her a squeeze then let go. "Have you eaten?"

"I tried but you see what happened."

"I could use a bit to eat." He caught her hand and led her toward the refreshment room.

Holding hands was such a lovely sensation. Much more intimate than one would guess. It made her feel truly married even though they had yet to share a bed.

For now they would share a meal...except that, as it turned out, she was the only one with an appetite.

When she had eaten a stuffed pigeon breast and was halfway finished with a slice of glazed ham, River begged to be excused. He'd spotted a business colleague with whom he had yet to speak.

It was beginning to seem as if being Viscount was a great deal of business and very little pleasure.

Having finished eating, Lilleth decided she ought to socialize, too.

She strolled about the ballroom. Oddly enough, she was in as much demand as River was. She could not walk six paces without ladies wishing to chat with Viscountess Aberly.

What she would rather do was dance with her husband.

Perhaps if River was finished speaking with his gentleman, she could convince him to.

A bit of fun would do him good.

Ah, there he was across the room. Smiling and anticipating her dance she walked toward him. Halfway around the perimeter of the dance floor she stopped abruptly. Lovely Alicia walked…or glided as it appeared…toward River.

Lilleth watched them speaking. What could they be saying to one another? And what would she not give to insert herself into the conversation.

It would be reassuring to know that her husband truly had no feelings for this lady he had once set aside. He'd told her that was not the case and she did believe him…

But then, they did not seem all that pleased to see one another. In fact, Mrs. Johnston patted her rounding middle, nodding if not smiling at whatever River had to say.

Then a tall man with a broad grin approached them. He kissed Alicia on the cheek then shook River's hand. The three of them spoke for a moment and then River glanced up and caught her looking at them.

Giving a quick goodbye, he hurried toward her.

"You've finished eating," he said. "We can go home if you are ready."

"What I am ready for is a dance with my husband."

His attitude softened; a small smile reached his eyes.

"I would enjoy a dance with my wife."

Waiting for the next piece of music to begin, Lilleth placed her hand in the crook of his arm. Every now and then his gaze shifted from the dancers to Alicia and her husband.

In Lilleth's opinion, the couple seemed very much in love.

"I imagine it was a surprise to see her so far from home?"

"Her?" River's eyebrows rose. "Mrs. Johnston, do you mean?"

"She is as lovely as you told me she was."

"Her husband has a time of it, I imagine, fending off her admirers."

The music started so she had no time to ask how he felt about seeing her after all this time. Pray that he was indifferent.

Then with the music swelling, River held her in his arms, smiled down at her. Suddenly, it was as if there was no one on the dance floor but the two of them.

There was every reason to have faith that she would win River's love. All it needed was a bit of perseverance.

Chapter Twelve

Lilleth watched River put on his coat then leave their hotel suite.

He had been quiet and withdrawn all day, which was a disappointment considering that last night after the matter of the mistress had been sorted out, they spent the evening smiling and in happy spirits.

Only one thing had kept her from dancing on air…one important thing. Other than that one time he'd held her hand, his touches had been either to do with dancing or escorting. There had been no lovely hints of romance whatsoever.

It seemed as if he was a brother more than a husband. And yet in unguarded moments she noticed that he was looking at her with a particular interest.

In those instants it was thrilling to feel his gaze circumspectly roaming over her person.

All evening she'd fantasized that he would secrete her away to a secluded corner and wrap her in an embrace and then kiss her the way she'd been waiting for.

A kiss that was no passing brush of lips, but one that was deep and sincere…one that a man gave his wife when…

Just imagining such a moment made her need to fan herself.

Drat it, the night had passed without her getting that kiss.

They were wed. She was willing. So why hadn't he?

River could be in no doubt of where her heart lay. When they'd bid one another good-night, she'd hinted that he would be welcome on the other side of her bedroom door.

Had she not felt the attraction between them, she might believe he simply did not wish to be intimate with a wife he had not chosen out of love.

Sometimes it seemed as if they were a pair of magnets, one moment attracting and another repelling.

What she needed was time alone to think matters over.

There was always something to do at Angel's Keep.

Mr. Gordon met her at the front door and helped her into her coat.

"Unsettled weather is brewing, my lady. I shall call for the carriage."

"No need to go to the trouble. I'm only walking a few blocks and I enjoy unsettled weather."

Moments later while descending in the elevator Lilleth peered down across the lobby. Through the big glass entry doors she saw the doorman's coattails flapping. Wind scattered leaves along the street.

The brisk walk heated her and by the time she came to the front door of Angel's Keep, she was not all that cold.

Surprisingly, the front the door was unlocked. Coming inside she saw a light shining from a back room.

What was that she heard?

River…singing?

It had been so long since she'd heard his beautiful voice. Since that night when they sang and danced together in the stable.

What would he do if she joined in? Stop probably, so she

stood in the hallway without making her presence known, simply listening.

Hearing his voice, so masculine and the song so full of longing, she thought…

She felt…

Warm.

But this heat had not a thing to do with the fireplace in the back room. Even with it, the building was not all that warm.

"River," she said softly, coming to stand in the doorway. "I'm here."

She took off her coat then lay it across the back of a chair.

River's song did not end abruptly, but slowly faded while he knelt on the floor next to an open paint can, watching her.

"Why are you here? Please say you did not walk. It's getting dark outside."

It was clear to her in an instant what she was doing here and it was not the same reason she'd had when she left the house.

Going out of the hotel, she'd needed a quiet place to think about how to deal with her chaste marriage. Now that she was here, she knew what to do about it…or try to.

"It's cold," she commented.

River reached for a log and then leaned sideways to add it to the fire. A soft orange glow brightened the walls for an instant.

A glow ignited within her, as well, but it was not soft.

"I figured I would do some painting," he told her.

"So I see."

Sitting on the chair where she'd draped her coat, she unlaced her shoes, slipped them off. Then with a fortifying breath she pressed toward her goal.

She rolled down her lacy garters, slipping her stockings off with them. She wiggled her toes…sighed.

She had never exposed her bare legs to a man.

Doing so made her feel bold, but at the same time soft and yielding.

Delightfully scandalous, too.

Yet there was no need to feel ill at ease over her immodesty. River was her husband, after all.

"What are you doing?" he asked.

It might only be fire glow reflecting on his face, but please let the flush have to do with her.

"I'm helping you paint."

"Your feet will get chilled," he said while offering her the extra brush.

"I don't believe they will."

River dipped his brush in the paint container. She dipped hers in at the same time, stirring slowly, drawing her fingers against his wrist, back and forth.

The motion seemed seductive to her, but she had no idea what his reaction would be.

"If you paint that wall—" he pointed to the one on the opposite side of the room "—I will finish this one."

That not being the reaction she hoped for, she gathered the courage to continue her bumbling seduction.

"I do not think so, River."

A bit of play seemed in order. Friskiness helped in every situation, did it not?

She knelt beside him…close beside. Then she dabbed a blot of paint on his nose.

"Playing with fire, Mrs. Halston?"

He dabbed one on her nose.

"I hope so."

She dropped her paintbrush in the can then plucked the brush from his hand and dropped it in, too.

"Is it war then?" he asked with a grin that seemed as intimate as a kiss.

Or perhaps it did not. A grin could be offered from a distance. A kiss could not be had without touching.

Shifting her weight, she boldly snuggled one knee between his muscular thighs and at the same time pressed her heart to his.

Delightfully face-to-face, there was no way he could misread her intentions. Nor could he move out of the way of her advance.

"I've captured you," she murmured then nuzzled his nose with hers.

And then she kissed him.

Her idea had been to give him a quick peck and coax him into a longer kiss.

That was not how it happened.

At the first sweep of her lips on his, he'd…cursed?

Surely not!

She must be mistaken because in the next second he yanked her closer and gave her a kiss so deep she felt her soul spin.

When he finally released her, she was all but gasping. So was he.

Apparently she had not captured him. They had captured one another.

A smear of white streaked from his nose to his cheek. She wiped it away with her thumb.

He wiped her face from nose to chin.

Tangling his hand in her hair, he drew her in for another

kiss. She was melting inside so she twined her fingers in his shirt to keep from sliding into a puddle on the floor.

Then, all at once, he let go of her.

"I'm sorry… I lost control for a moment."

Lost control? Lost? Control?

Why would he not want to? The intimacy unfolding between them had been too long in coming as it was.

Did he not wish for her to become his wife in the truest sense? How else were they to begin a family? From all she had observed over the years, there was no other way for it to happen.

But… *I'm sorry?*

Those softly spoken words crushed her.

The only thing that she was sorry for was…nothing.

"You got paint in my hair," she accused, grasping for something to say.

"My apologies." With lowered brows, he brushed the spot with his thumb.

"What I do not have is paint on that wall." She snatched her brush out of the can, then scooted to the wall she had been assigned to paint.

She might sound nettled and she was. But more than that she was bewildered. How could she have misread his feelings so horribly?

Clearly she had, though. Irritated at herself and at him, she slapped paint on the wall with greater vigor than was called for.

"I'm sorry, Lilleth," he said again.

"If you say that one more time I shall…" Weep? Later she would but not now. "Dump the bucket of paint on your head."

"I should not have taken advantage of you."

"You did not. I was quite willing."

If it took all she had she was not going to allow him to see her snuffle and blink tears.

"As you may have noticed, I was the one to have begun the seduction." Slapping a jagged line of paint on the plaster she added, "Which you rejected."

Baffled and frustrated, she flicked her brush at him.

"That is fair payment for getting paint in my hair."

"Perhaps we should continue later," he suggested.

"Continue what later?"

"Painting this room." He set his brush aside, braced his hands on his thighs.

River Halston had distracting hands.

Which he clearly meant to keep to himself.

"Very well," she paused in her attack on the wall. "We will continue painting later. Right now we will discuss why you reject me as your wife?"

Rather than answer, he picked at a loose thread on his shirt.

"I have a right to know," she pressed.

In the face of his continued interest in the thread, she presented the only argument that made sense.

"It is because you are in love with Alicia?"

There, it was out in the open to be denied by him or accepted by her.

"That is not true." At least he was no longer worrying at the thread. "You saw how happy she and her husband are."

"They are expecting a child, so yes, they do look happy."

Lilleth on the other hand might never have that joy if River continued to spurn her.

She did not tell him that, though. She had no wish to say hurtful things to him. Once spoken, words could not be taken back. They were like needles in the heart, forever wounding. No, until she was in control of her emotions, it would be better not to speak.

But then…

"How many children do you want?"

He glanced away.

"I want as many as our home will fit," she told him. "If the estate house is large, then it will be quite a few."

"One. I—"

She wagged her brush at him in order to press her point. "I had two brothers. Both of them died. I was left without siblings. I will not have any child grow up alone, Lord Aberly."

With a huff of frustration, she set her brush aside, rose from the floor and stomped over to the chair. Sitting, she crossed her legs then rolled her stockings on, securing them with a snap of her lacy garters.

An odd look crossed River's face. She did not dare confuse it with desire for her. Very likely it was the paint streak making his expression look like what it was not.

"Surely you do not believe in the heir and spare absurdity." She put on her shoes, looking across at him while she yanked the laces.

His glance slid away. Stifling a groan, he stood up.

"You do believe it!"

"There is much you do not understand."

His silence indicated that he was not going to enlighten her.

"No child of mine will be a spare. Probably not an heir either if he is to live by the rules which bind you."

She yanked on her coat and did not bother to say goodbye. Later, at bedtime, she would not tell him good-night, either.

Going outside, she paced down the sidewalk at a brisk

pace wishing she had accepted the offer of the carriage. It was so cold she feared her teeth would clack.

She heard footsteps coming up fast from behind.

Glancing over her shoulder she saw River, his shoulders hunched against the chill and his strides long.

Here was a man who made no sense whatsoever.

For someone who only wished to father boys…and only two of them, he was certainly fond of his three nieces.

It did not take long for him to catch up with her, to catch her elbow and look hard into her eyes.

"I meant to speak of the matter of children sooner, but I never found the opportune moment. Please forgive me."

Truly? He'd simply not gotten to it? To her this was a matter of critical importance. Evidently it was not to him.

"Boy children do you mean? Would a girl…or a few of them be such a burden to you?"

"That is not what I meant."

"How am I to know what you mean since you chose not to tell me."

"We should get home before you catch a chill."

Too late for that, she'd already gotten a chill. It gripped her heart, squeezed without mercy.

"Were your parents in love?" she asked.

He stopped walking quite suddenly, seeming startled at the question, which was a reasonable one.

"Why would you ask?"

"Because I need to understand why you will not allow me here." She tapped his chest, felt his heart beating hard and quick. "If your parents had a destructive marriage, then I might understand how you would be frightened of having the same."

"They did love one another." His words formed cold

mist in the air between them. "And that is what made the marriage destructive."

"That makes no sense, River."

"It does when nothing existed for them beyond their chamber door."

"And Aberly came to ruin because of it?"

While his logic made little sense to her, clearly, he had been damaged by his parent's example.

"You are not your father." She touched his cheek, her resentment weakened by love. "I am not your mother."

For all that her husband held mulishly to outrageous notions, she did in fact love him.

And Heaven help her for it.

"Come, we will freeze if we stand here a moment longer." He lay his arm across her shoulder, drawing her in.

With a twist of her shoulder, she shrugged him off.

"You are shivering. I merely wish to warm you."

"You cannot."

Because it was not the weather causing her chill.

Loving a man who would not love her back? That was what made her shiver.

There was nothing she could do to warm herself against a bleak future.

River stomped back and forth over the rug in his chamber berating himself for all he had done…or more to the point, not done to create this mess with his wife.

One moment he had been satisfied with his friendly marriage, and the next he was kissing Lilleth as if he had his heart to give her.

What he should have done was inform her of his wishes on the matter of intimacy and children on the day they wed.

No, before they wed.

It would have been the fair thing to do, but he'd needed to marry her and she'd needed to marry him. Back then it did not seem such a big matter.

Now, though, he had made a mess of things and did not know how to make them right.

The last thing he wished was to make Lilleth unhappy. He owed her much…everything to be honest. However, he did not owe her his heart.

Had he indulged in kissing her for a moment longer tonight, she would have had it.

It was awfully quiet in her bedroom.

Good, she was not weeping.

But what was she doing? Sleeping soundly while he paced?

He pressed his ear to the door.

Nothing.

The door had never been locked between them so he inched it open.

He did wish to smooth matters over between them if he could.

"Lilleth," he whispered softly, not wishing to startle her awake. "Lilleth…"

Slowly, he opened the door.

She was not in bed. Not in the chair by the window, either.

Making a quick search of the other rooms in the suite, he did not find her.

"Curse it," he muttered while pressing his nose to the windowpane in the main room and trying to spot her down in the garden.

Hopefully she was not sitting on a garden bench. High wind was lashing shrubs so violently that it looked as if they might uproot and sail all the way to the stable.

The stable! Of course, that would be where she was. It was where he went for solace and he knew she did the same.

She would seek the comfort of being with her horse. It did not make him feel best proud of himself as a husband knowing his wife turned to an animal for consolation rather than him.

But since he was the source of her misery why did he think she would…or that he could help?

What he could do was make certain she was safe.

Going to his bedroom, he snatched a blanket off the bed.

Wrapping the thick quilt around his shoulders he went outside, using the back stairway.

A time or two the wind nearly pulled the blanket out of his grip, but he held on tight.

He did not know for certain she that was cold, but in the event, the quilt would help. Another husband, a better one, would heat his wife with his body.

A better husband would not have driven his bride to the stable.

The fact remained that he could not touch her as said better husband would do. Tonight he'd learned how easily he could get carried away when it came to his bride.

If he had not gotten control of himself earlier, he would have handed his heart over along with his body.

One thing was certain, he must not risk being intimate with her again.

A gust of wind whooshed around his head cold enough to make his ears ache.

It felt as if the remainder of fall had given way to winter.

What if he did not find Lilleth in the stable? Where would she have gone? Home perhaps? To Apple Valley Acres?

It was unlikely at this time of night.

"Curse it!" He didn't mumble this time since the wind would catch his cussing and blow it to who knew where.

For good measure he cursed again, because wouldn't Society have a grand time gossiping about how he had wed in New York but come home without a bride?

Thinking back to the time he had written that first letter to Lilleth, the matter of marriage had seemed uncomplicated.

He would wed, give the lady his name and she would give him her money. Life would go on much as it had, with him performing his duties as Viscount and his wife fulfilling hers as Viscountess.

Everything he had believed back then turned out to be wrong. There was not a chance that his wife was going to go her own way.

Nor, in truth, did he want her to. She'd taken her place in the family. He could no longer imagine her not being a part of it. Clara adored her and so did his nieces.

There was no reason why he and Lilleth could not found their marriage on friendship…deep friendship even.

Except that he was lying to himself. He did see a reason.

She needed what he could not give her.

Coming around the corner to where the Aberly horses were housed, he spotted the stall where Arrow now resided with the other horses he owned.

He peeked over the door and there she was, asleep on a heap of straw with only a thin blanket to cover her.

Going inside, he placed the quilt over her then stooped down to tuck it about her shoulders.

He brushed strands of golden hair from her cheek.

There were dried tear tracks on her face. What a cad he was to have put them there.

Sunshine souls should never cry. Or shiver, which was what she was doing in her sleep.

The thin blanket she'd huddled under was not adequate for any sort of warmth.

The right thing to do would be wake her, insist she come back inside the hotel. But being asleep, she was no longer weeping.

"All right then, Sleeping Beauty."

And a beauty, she was. Not as stunning as Alicia was but far more beautiful.

How was he to beget his heir without losing himself to her?

Once again he tucked the quilt around her, more slowly this time because his fingers lingered at the dip of her waist and stalled on the swell of her hips.

He could not recall being more frightened of anyone in his life.

It was a lucky thing that stable hands were on call at all hours. The last thing he needed was to be alone with Lilleth right now.

There were a few stoves lit but it was still cooler in this stall. Lanterns kept the space from being too dark.

A red plaid blanket hung on a wall peg so he snatched it and then sat against a hay bale. He drew the scratchy wool over himself. It was smelly but also warm.

Having the extra quilt, it took only a moment for Lilleth to quit shivering.

Somehow, he would need to make peace between them but was not sure how to go about it.

One thing was for certain, it would not happen if he told her how deeply he'd loved the woman he had put aside in order to marry her. And how because of it, he refused to love again.

He ought to have told her the truth from the beginning, but now, having denied it, he could not.

How was a man to tell his wife that love was simply not meant for a man like him.

The cursed truth of the matter was, it was meant for a woman like Lilleth.

"You scare me," he murmured.

Like nothing ever had. Without meaning to, she threatened all he needed to keep safe…she and her fortune being among them.

Leaning back against a rough post, he closed his eyes certain that he would not sleep.

The next he knew, grooms were going about their early morning chores. Someone had placed the quilt over him.

Lilleth was gone.

Chapter Thirteen

Two weeks had passed since Lilleth tried and failed to seduce her husband.

Nothing had changed overmuch during that time except that the weather had turned unseasonably warm. People out on their strolls left their heavy coats behind in favor of taking in the sunshine.

She and River were cordial, but not easy with one another as they had been before she forced herself upon him.

The truth she must accept was that she would not have the marriage she'd hoped for. River could not give her what he did not have.

Smiles for one thing. Mr. Sullen was keeping those to himself. Even his nieces had to work for them.

Luckily Lilleth's days were busy. There were visits with ladies of new and old money, as well as the required shopping to be done.

Only a few details remained to be finished before the opening of the orphanage.

Nights were as busy as days. As much as she wished for time to relax, each night brought a new social event. She hoped that once they went to London, life would get slower.

Not that going to the theater, the opera and dinner parties was so awful. Those were the times she was escorted on River's arm. She was free to touch him in the name of presenting the image of a happy newlywed couple.

Judging by the smiles cast their way, people believed them to be what they appeared.

One of those people was her…sometimes. A fulfilling marriage was not all that hard to imagine.

With River so close, she could smell the man under the cologne. Other times, she watched his lips while he spoke and remembered how it was to kiss them. And remembering, she felt a bubble of hope rising.

Sadly, it always burst before she could fully catch it.

Could she really have been so utterly mistaken about what was happening between them?

Apparently she could be.

But never mind. Tonight would be another event where she would touch him and pretend.

Mrs. Martin was presenting her daughter's vocal talent in a musicale at her home on 5th Avenue.

While sitting on a stool and watching her maid style her hair, Lilleth wondered if tonight was the night her husband would look at her in a different way…as if she were Emily again.

At a soft knock on the bedroom door, her maid hurried across the room to answer but Deborah entered first, looking elegant and dressed for the evening's musicale.

"Oh, my dear, there is a note sent to you from that nice man who is fixing up Angel's Keep. I imagine he is undecided about what color to paint the window trim."

Note delivered, Aunt Deborah hurried back out of the room.

Millie, the lady's maid, returned to fuss with the last curl. After it was set, she helped Lilleth into her gown.

Once Millie went out of the room, Lilleth picked up the note from where she had set it on the bedside table.

Mr. Beale did tend to feel that each detail of design was urgent so she had not rushed to read it.

Humming, she unfolded the note.

"Two orphans have been dropped at the door. Come quickly before my ears are damaged from their ceaseless screeching."

Orphans at the door! Now?

Clearly the musicale would have to go on without her. Setting the note on the table, she snatched up her coat and rushed out of the bedroom.

There would be so many people present to admire Miss Martin's voice, Lilleth's applause would not be missed. Small children needed to be settled in and comforted; that was where her duty lay.

"Oh, you are still here, my lady! I thought you'd already gone to the lobby to meet the family at the ice swan," Millie exclaimed.

"If anyone asks, please let them know I was needed at Angel's Keep."

She took the back stairs because going across the garden and past the stables was the quickest way to the orphanage.

She was hardly alone on the street. Dozens of conveyances carried people to elegant gatherings.

Viscountess Aberly would not be among them tonight.

Hurrying up the walkway, she heard babies crying before she even opened the door.

The carriage had been brought around to the front of the hotel. River's nieces bounced on the seats happy to have been invited to play with their hostess's children, but

Clara and Aunt Deborah peered at him through the windows looking concerned.

He gave them a nod to assure them they would soon be on their way.

Where was Lilleth? She was always punctual.

He rushed back inside the hotel not waiting for the doorman to assist then jogged up the main stairway.

What could possibly be delaying her? According to Deborah, Lilleth's maid had only to add a few touches to her hair.

There was nothing for it but to go and bring her down.

Coming into the main room he did not see her, but her scent lingered. It filled his nose, his lungs…and as much as he resisted the draw, it filled his heart.

She must have taken the elevator down while he raced up the stairs. But it was unsettling not to know where she was…again.

Was she so dissatisfied in the marriage that she had gone home? It was far from unheard-of for a woman to flee an unhappy marriage. He was too aware that what she wanted he could not give her.

Of course his imagination was running away with him. Lilleth would not abandon them without a word.

Nonetheless, unfounded worry presented an image of life without his wife and it plunged his heart to his gut.

Standing alone in her bedroom he had the same bleak feeling that he'd had when he'd sent Alicia away.

But then, it could not be the same feeling because he'd been in love with Alicia and he was not with Lilleth.

Millie came into the room carrying an armload of clean towels.

"Oh, good, there you are, my lord. Lady Aberly said to tell you she needed to go to the orphanage."

What an idiot he'd been to briefly entertain the thought that she left him.

Going away without a word was simply not something she would do.

But what had come up at Angel's Keep that required her attention so suddenly?

River went back downstairs, sent the carriage along to the musicale, then walked toward Angel's Keep.

Within moments he was coming up the walkway.

Whatever had happened could not be so horrible because a lullaby ushered soothingly from the other side of the door.

Coming inside he found his wife kneeling on the floor in front of the hearth, the warm glow of the fire outlining her form while she cradled a sleeping baby.

Her song, however, was directed at another baby lying on a blanket beside her.

It kicked its small legs, gazing up and gurgling in the charming way he recalled his nieces doing.

Lilleth glanced up at him, all the while carrying on with the lullaby.

Something inside him went soft. He got the oddest sensation that this was what his future could be. Lilleth would give him this, if only he was willing.

Despite the voice of caution whispering in his mind, he crouched down, smiled at Lilleth and then the kicking baby.

"They arrived early," she told him.

"Girls or boys?"

"One of each. Twins. Their older brother brought them in."

"What happened to their parents?"

"Their mother died giving birth to them. The father died before he even knew about them. Their brother took care of them for a time with the help of an elderly neighbor.

There was no money so he went to work in a factory. But then the neighbor could not handle the babies on her own so here they are."

"Which one is this?" he asked reaching for the child on the blanket. He'd forgotten how good it felt to hold a baby.

"The little girl…her name is Janie. This little boy is Peter."

"And how old is your older brother, Miss Janie?" he cooed to the baby, but of course it was Lilleth he expected an answer from.

"Fifteen or so, I would guess. He left here weeping, River. He wants them. I told him he could come back to visit whenever he wishes."

"He sounds like a reliable lad. We need staff. There is no reason we cannot hire him."

"No reason at all. His name is Matthew. He's coming back in the morning. You may ask him then."

"I will. It appears that I'll need to ask the rest of the staff to begin work earlier than they planned to as well."

For a time they sat on the floor rocking babies, neither of them speaking.

Flames in the hearth burned warm. A log fell, sparks snapped.

"These are the lucky ones." Lilleth stroked Peter's wispy-looking hair. "Thanks to their brother we got them before they were neglected."

"Angel's Keep was a brilliant idea, my dear."

She smiled at him while snuggling the baby closer.

While as beautiful as always, this was not her usual smile. He felt a message behind it.

"I have many good ideas," she answered, her voice all but a sigh.

Opening his mouth he meant to ask what they were. But then he knew.

His wife was not speaking of improvements to Angel's Keep.

This could be theirs, was what her eyes told him.

Their hearth, their children…a family bound in love…

She had spoken no words to entice him. All she did was look at him.

He'd heard of tasting fear and in this moment he understood it.

"I know what you are thinking," he said, his heart scrambling for purchase. "Once we reach London we should open another establishment like Angel's Keep."

She shook her head, continued to smile at him in that secret, knowing way. "Yes, we will, but that is not at all what I was thinking."

And then she kissed the baby's cheek and began to sing.

Doing so, she'd impressed an image in his mind. One which both repelled and drew him.

It was of Lilleth riding her horse across the green pastures of Apple Valley Acres. She was spinning a rope slowly over her head…a lasso it was. When she let go, it sailed through the sky then came to rest…around his ribs.

In the vision, not only had she captured his heart, but his future.

A future having half a dozen babies born of love, not obligation.

This, however, could not be. His responsibility to Aberly came before anything else.

Once before through lack of attention he had nearly lost everything. He would not risk it happening again.

There would be but one or two children if things went

as he planned them. He could lose himself…his heart, if he allowed more.

In a choice between losing his heart or keeping Aberly, he must choose Aberly. A viscount's duty came before all else.

And yet, his affection for Lilleth was genuine. He could not say she did not hold a part of his heart.

A part which Alicia had never held. A better part, maybe.

When had he ever danced with Alicia in a barn or sang with her? Or visited a cemetery by the light of a full moon? When had she ever offered him two mistresses and made him laugh so hard his sides ached?

Never. Looking back, he realized that he and Alicia had never had much fun.

Which went to prove what he believed to be true.

Friendship was better than romance.

An idea came to him which would prove it once and for all.

"The weather has turned warm. We should take advantage of it while we can. What do you say we have a bit of fun tomorrow, just the two of us?"

"Have you forgotten the family is leaving for the ranch in the morning?"

He had forgotten. He'd meant to use the quiet days with them gone to get work done. He had one especially important meeting the day after next that, if successful, would ensure the financial stability of Aberly for years to come.

"Another time, then," he said, surprised at how disappointed he was.

"What sort of fun did you have in mind?"

"I thought we could take the horses out for a ride in Central Park…lunch at Delmonico's?"

"Or a picnic in the park? I would consider missing a trip home for that."

"Done. A picnic it is."

Tomorrow would be proof that fun with Lilleth was better than romance with Alicia.

He would have the marriage he'd hoped for.

Morning dawned as bright and lovely as a day could be.

Lilleth's spirits echoed the sunshine filtering through the trees of Central Park.

Because what did spending time "just the two of us" mean to him?

That she would finally have the marriage she had hoped for?

He was certainly the man she had hoped for and there was no denying it.

And one day he would love her. Seeing the way he was looking at her now, his hair tossed and ruffled in a rising breeze, his eyes aglow with pleasure, how could it not be true?

Here was the River that Emily knew. This morning he was not hiding behind the wall he'd put up between them.

Women's intuition, which Mama claimed to be a very real thing especially when it came to one's husband, told her he was close to falling in love with her.

The ride was glorious. Sometimes they laughed, exchanging stories about the nieces. Other times they spoke of his plans to bring prosperity to Aberly. With pride and affection he told her about his country home and about the town house in London.

Before long they were deep into the park.

She hadn't even noticed a bank of black clouds building

on the horizon. Others park goers must have paid better attention for the crowds had thinned.

"Let's have lunch under this huge tree," she suggested. "Are you hungry?"

"I only hope there is enough food for both of us." His quick grin was nothing less than a challenge.

What a wonderful smile he had. She would never grow tired of seeing it. It was more delectable than the cakes she'd spotted in the food basket.

While they ate and spoke of this and that, the air cooled, but the sun was bright and threatening clouds remained on the horizon.

"I could take a nap in this spot and not wake for hours," River stretched and yawned.

"But wouldn't you rather climb this tree and have a magnificent view of the park?"

"It would be something to see, risky, though."

"Do not tell me you afraid of falling?" she teased.

"I'm afraid of you falling."

"Ha! I've been climbing trees all my life. I am as agile as a squirrel."

"Those were my brother's exact words a second before he fell out of a tree we were exploring and broke his arm."

"Luckily I am not your brother." For more reasons than she would explain. "I challenge you to a contest. Let's see who can climb the highest."

"No."

"Is that fear I smell?"

"It's caution." He stretched on the grass looking as if he would take that nap.

"Very well, a person cannot be too cautious."

Lilleth got up and retrieved a rope from her saddle pack.

She dangled it across his nose. "I will tie you to me so you will not fall."

"You carry a rope with you?" He batted it away from his face then sat up.

"Of course I do. Back on the ranch everyone does. It is a useful piece of equipment."

"As you wish, then." He stood up. With his wonderful grin flashing, he tied them together at the waist, leaving enough slack in the rope to allow for climbing. "Prepare to be defeated, Lilleth."

With the branches sturdy and well spaced, it was an easy climb and well worth the effort.

As it turned out, she was defeated, but what she felt was victorious.

Perched about fifteen feet off the ground they sat side by side, swinging their legs and enjoying a view of treetops beginning to take fall color.

Life was delightful.

She thought of kissing him. The mood seemed right, but then again, she had been mistaken about it before. It was a long fall if things did not go as her imagination pictured.

"Was that thunder?" she asked, hearing a faint rumble.

"I hope not—those children are having far too much fun to have to quit their game."

"So am I." She reached for River's hand, gave it a squeeze.

"Me too. I enjoy your company very much, Lilleth." He squeezed her hand back. "I look forward to…That one was thunder. We need to get down at once."

He was right, trees and lightning were a dangerous mix, but what was he looking forward to?

All at once rain slapped the leaves. How had those wicked-looking clouds blown over without her noticing?

Down below the few people who remained in the park scattered.

"You make a start. I'll be right behind with this useful rope to hold you if you slip," he said.

"If I do you'll probably come down on top of me."

She hadn't yet reached the ground when a deluge crashed, making the tree seem like a waterfall.

All she could see was water where grass ought to be. It would be a wonder if the picnic basket had not washed away.

Her foot touched the ground.

"I'm down," she called up but wondered if he could hear her over the racket the rain made.

Seconds later, River stood beside her.

"Thunder sounds closer." He snatched her hand and ran for the horses, kicking aside the picnic basket, which was in his way.

Sloshing water made it seem like she was running on glass.

She fell hard on her bottom side.

River scooped her up in the very instant a blaze of light blanched the area.

The horses pranced and pulled on their tethers but calmed when River spoke soothingly to them.

Lilleth turned, started to mount Arrow.

"Ooof," the breath rushed out of her. How could she have forgotten about the rope?

She tried to untie the knot, but the wet hemp was too difficult to loosen.

"No time for that. The storm front is moving toward us fast."

That said, he tied his horse's reins to Arrow's saddle pack then tossed her up onto her horse's back.

For a second the roped pinched her waist but then River leaped up behind her and the tension eased.

Eased from the rope, but not from her husband. The arms braced around her were rigid. There was no mistaking that the need to get back to the hotel was urgent.

In a short time they were out of the park and racing down the middle of 5th Avenue. The street was deserted by now and the clatter of their horses' hooves echoed off buildings.

When they finally reached the stable the storm was nearly overhead.

River helped her down, called for a stable boy then handed off the animals to him.

"Let's go," he caught her hand, rushing her toward the door.

"Shouldn't you cut us free first?"

"No time. Another minute and it will be too risky to cross the garden."

A series of cracks and flashes warned he was right.

No sooner had he ushered her into the hotel's back stairwell than a lightning bolt hit the garden fountain.

Thunder shook the hotel walls. Lilleth heard someone shriek.

No one was home when they got to their suite. River opened the nearest door and brought her into the study where they would be alone, but the hearth was cold and Lilleth was shivering.

"Don't worry, I'll have a fire going in no time."

Far quicker than if he rang for help.

"We are safe at home and just in time. You are my hero."

He did not feel like a hero, but it was flattering to hear.

Tied to one another they crossed to the hearth. River put in kindling, stacked logs and then lit a match.

He sat on the floor, drawing Lilleth down beside him while they waited for warmth.

It did not take long. Soon heat rolled out of the fireplace in a wave of comfort.

To hurry the warmth along, he held Lilleth's icy fingers and rubbed them between his palms.

"Isn't this a bit of heaven?"

"Something like it, I think," he answered, glad he'd married a woman who spoke good over a situation rather than complaining about it. "Now, let's get out of these wet clothes."

He tried to unfasten the buttons of his shirt, but stiff fingers made him clumsy.

All at once there was another pair of hands working his buttons.

"A wife's job is to be helpful." She bit her bottom lip to prevent a smile, but it didn't help much. Her eyes were laughing.

Clearly she saw humor in his predicament.

The problem was, she would need to undress, too. It was not as if she could seek the privacy of her bedroom to do it.

Looking at matters now, he ought to have taken a moment to have the stableman cut the rope.

Although it was common for husbands and wives to be unclothed in the presence of one another, it was not common for Lilleth and him.

How was he to resist the temptation his wife presented?

He was a strong-willed man, but even for him, being tied to a desirable woman who was at this exact instant drawing his shirt off of his shoulders presented too great an enticement.

It might help if she was not so obviously enjoying seeing his bare skin pebble.

The fact that he was wed to her made matters all the more treacherous.

"Which is absurd," he mumbled.

"Quite absurd," his wife answered.

Chapter Fourteen

"How do you know what I find absurd?"

He crossed his arms over his chest giving Lilleth a glance that she judged to be somewhere between bemused and annoyed.

What, she wondered, must he be seeing in hers? The image he presented did not lend itself to chaste thoughts.

But she did have an idea what he was struggling with. This was not the first time she'd seen him fighting with himself when it came to indulging in intimate moments.

"You find it absurd that you are not reaching over to unbutton my shirt." She began to do it herself, noting that he watched every flick of her fingers. "You are right, River, it is absurd."

She wiggled her arms out of her blouse then took it off and spread it on the floor in front of the fireplace.

Her chemise was also wet but given his hesitation, she decided to let it dry while she wore it.

"River Halston." She touched his cheek. It felt deliciously stubbled against her palm. "I am your wife. No rules will be broken here tonight if you touch me."

He opened his mouth, closed it, then shook his head. But then he took her hand, kissed her fingers…

And then gave her hand back to her!

"You are bound to me by a rope and it is useless to try and escape," she told him.

He gave a slow sigh. "It's not only the rope."

With that he slipped his fingers under the knot at her waist and tugged her to him.

Then he kissed her mouth, tangled his fingers in her wet hair.

Her skin had grown so cold that she nearly recoiled from the heat of his chest.

But of course she did not. She pressed closer.

Then all at once he set her away, looked up at the ceiling as if seeking a leak. Although rain pounded incessantly, not a single drop got through.

"We need scissors." His eyes shifted to the window where rain sluicing off the eaves resembled a waterfall.

"Look at me, River…tell me why you do not want me." Truthfully, she was not sure how much more she could take of his fickle ardor.

Sizzling then icy…it was enough to make a viscountess lose her composure.

He jerked his gaze back to her.

"It must be clear that I do want you, but it is not a simple thing for me."

"What could be simpler than a man wanting his wife and a wife wanting her husband?"

Not a single thing.

"For me there is nothing simple about it. As Viscount I have many people's well-being to think of. I am not my own."

"That is such nonsense I do not know how to argue it."

"Then do not. Just understand that I cannot allow myself to become distracted by…by matters of…" He pointed his thumb back and forth between them. “Men who do not put business first ruin their titles.”

“And you know this because you’ve done it before?” she asked even knowing he would never act irresponsibly.

“I told you about my father…how he nearly ruined Aberly. But I am partly to blame since I was oblivious to what he was doing.”

“Unless you were amusing yourself with your mistress at the time, it is illogical to make the comparison. And how many mistresses have you had, River?”

Five full seconds passed while he narrowed his eyes at her, pressed his lips in a tight seam.

“I was not involved with a mistress. You know how I feel on that matter.”

“I know what you have told me. But as matters stand now, I am more confused than I was before you tried to explain this.”

Was it truly possible for a man to look at her as if he wanted to devour her and then set her away as if she meant nothing to him at all?

A cold fellow with no heart might do that, but her husband was not that man.

The fire had warmed the small room and her thin chemise was beginning to dry and become less revealing. And a good thing, too. The last thing she wished for was to be sitting here with her wifely charms on display while her husband explained why he did not want her…or perhaps did but would not act on it.

If she was not anchored to him by this rope, she would march off to her bedroom.

“We need to cut this.” She started to rise but he caught the tether and drew her back down.

"First, I need for you to understand my position. That I care for you but..."

"Well, Mr. High and Mighty Viscount, I do not understand it. What you must understand, is that I believe you have shackled yourself with a stupid belief."

"Stupid?" His eyes went wide, his brows rose.

Very likely, no one had ever had the temerity to speak the truth so bluntly to his lofty self.

Lilleth Halston was not "no one." She was his wife.

And so, "Foolish, if you will, then. Pointless? Idiotic and crackbrained?"

All of those suited him, River decided.

What she did not realize was that he was frightened in a way he had never been.

His legally wed wife was sitting only inches away, wearing a shift that, although drying, was still revealing.

He was indeed stupid if all he did was sit and stare.

"You scare me," he whispered leaning closer, adding the scent of her skin to the temptation he was succumbing to.

"I'm not scaring you, River. You are scaring yourself," she whispered inching closer to him.

Lilleth touched his shoulder, trailed her fingers down his chest and tugged at the binding knot.

"You have no important business to attend to tonight that might be jeopardized, therefore I propose a test."

"What sort of test?" His heart beat hard, his blood ran hotter all of a sudden.

"Take me properly...make me your wife in every way. If Aberly falls to ruin it will prove you are right. If it does not, then—"

Then he would be free to love her.

He whispered an endearment against her lips but was

not sure what. Somehow it got lost between his brain and his mouth.

He pressed her gently to the rug, kissed her as if he was a starving man released at a banquet.

No more. He meant to indulge in his marriage…in his beautiful wife.

Surely she was right and nothing that happened between now and tomorrow would harm the estate.

He thought…no was certain, that loving Lilleth would make it better. Perhaps even result in his heir.

When she gave herself over to him, to his touches and his kisses…when she gave them back to him, he was—

Lost?

Or was it found?

Bound was what he was, and not by the rope.

The very thing he'd determined would not happen, had.

He was in love with his wife.

And glad of it.

River may have been hesitant to give all of himself to their marriage, but given what the past several hours had revealed, Lilleth believed he no longer was.

The fear he'd harbored when it came to her had vanished. Every touch and kiss had proved him to be committed to their marriage. Fully surrendered and nothing less.

A sacred bond had been formed between them. He hadn't told her he loved her, not with words, but there was an unspoken language between them tonight which declared it quite clearly.

The heart knew what the heart knew.

Lilleth wriggled out of her husband's sleepy embrace. She sat up, added another log to the fireplace.

The flame had not ignited before she felt River's large

hand curl around her arm. With a grunt, he drew her back down to the rug and pulled her close.

"It's still raining." She listened to the wind huff against the windows.

"Makes no difference to us," he murmured into the sweat-dampened curls at her temple. "We are home."

She stretched her arms over her head, felt the carpet tickle her back. It was so nice lying bare in front of the fire, she wondered if they would even make it to his bed.

She could never have imagined the vigor that went into marital pleasure.

Now, before she had fully regained her energy, they were giving and taking love once again.

It was an hour later when she noticed that the drying rope was chafing her bare skin.

"We really should find something to cut this with," she said, but not wanting to rise from where they were in order to do it.

"You are right."

With a frown he gazed at the red marks on her skin. She pointed to the raw marks on his.

"Don't worry, it was worth it," she told him and, oh, how true it was.

"We'll heal." River returned her grin then stood up and reached his hand down to her. "Let's look over on my desk."

They walked across the room as bare as newly hatched starlings.

Lilleth felt free in a way she never had. At last, there was nothing between her and her husband. Their hearts were joined as completely as their bodies had been.

River opened his desk drawer. "Look at that, scissors right on top."

"River Halston! You knew they were there all along."

"I was distracted. My mind was muddled. But I'm glad I forgot about them."

The blades must have been sharp. They cut through the rope easily.

"I'm glad, too. But now that we are not forced to be together, what shall we do with our freedom?" she asked.

"Same thing as before." He kissed her nose, her cheek and then her lips. "Only in different places."

He held her by the waist then lifted her off the floor and set her on his desk.

"Oh…well, yes, this will be…"

She did not know exactly the words to describe what. Luckily he showed her without speaking.

After that, the chair next to his desk proved to be highly entertaining with lightning flashes blazing through the window and turning the shade of their skin from flushed to beached white.

Much later, although she had no idea what time, close to dawn perhaps, River took her to his bed where they became a tangle of arms, legs and contented sighs.

River was the first one to fall asleep.

Spooning into him, she listened to wind blow and howl, to rain beating heavily on the roof.

She had never been more content in her life. This sense of well-being was not like anything she'd ever known. She did not want to sleep and miss a second of it.

Morning would come, Aberly would still be solvent and she would have her husband every night from now on.

After a moment River began to snore. The soft rise and fall of the sound lulled her. She fell asleep dreaming of moving her belongings into her husband's bedroom.

She did not know another thing until urgent banging pounded the door of the hotel suite.

* * *

River sat up with a jolt.

Someone was pounding the daylights out of the door.

Glancing at the window he saw that the storm had passed. A wide beam of sunshine streamed into the room touching his wife's hair as if it were a halo.

What could anyone want this early in the morning? After last night his mind was too fuzzy to make sense of it.

He stepped into his pants and hobbled toward the main room. The knocking continued.

"Viscount Aberly!"

Mr. Levitt!

He yanked the door open, staring at the grave expression on his solicitor's face.

"What time is it?" River asked with a sick feeling cramping his stomach.

"Too late for your meeting. Mr. Wilcox waited for two hours. When he departed he was in a temper. I'm afraid he has changed his mind about doing business with you."

Time and life stood still for the briefest second while he went utterly cold inside.

Pivoting on his heel, he walked back to his bedroom. Lilleth stretched and blinked her eyes open.

"I have missed my meeting," he stated while dressing as hastily as possible. "I must see what is to be done about this mistake."

He must look like a stone since it was how he felt.

"Last night was not a mistake," she called after him as he dashed into the main room. "You will find your way around this."

Not a mistake?

It was the most colossal blunder he had ever made.

Catching up with Mr. Levitt in the hallway, River understood something he had not before.

Loving Alicia had been no more than infatuation. One which he had clung to for far too long. The wound he'd believed he'd suffered when she wed another was no more than a scratch. And that to his ego more than his heart.

Loving Lilleth was a wound he would carry forever.

She had been so certain her challenge would prove her to be in the right.

For several hours, the best ones of his life, he'd believed her.

Now he must put his heart away. Become, again, the man who understood that business was what mattered.

Here was his proof that love in marriage was not meant for a man like him.

He'd failed Aberly in the exact way he had feared. The odds of him making amends for this mistake were slim. Important men had their choice of investors.

Lilleth had told him he would find a way around this.

She was wrong. Even if he did manage to reschedule this meeting, which was unlikely, there would always be other meetings.

There was no way around the fact that his life from now on would be a continual battle between duty and loving his wife.

Hours after River went out, Lilleth watched through her chamber window while people strolled about the garden taking in welcome sunshine.

She was not blissfully moving her belongings into her husband's bedroom.

Nor was she gazing out her chamber window in a fit of tears.

Looking back, it had been a mistake to issue the challenge as she had. She had known how important River's meeting was to him.

How, though, could she possibly have guessed how the night would go? Nothing she had ever witnessed at the ranch had prepared her for what happened between a husband and wife.

Mother had never told her about it and farm animals were a poor example.

Loving River had been the most wonderful surprise of her life even though it had come crashing about her head in the end.

There was nothing about it she would change…except for issuing a challenge.

All it ended up doing was convincing River he was right when really, he was wrong. Terribly wrong.

The intimacy they shared proved she had the right of the issue.

She cupped her chin in her hand, tapped her fingers on her lips.

River had not told her he loved her…not in an outright declaration. But surely he did. His heart had spoken. Her heart had heard it.

There was but one thing to do. Overcome this ridiculous idea of his by ignoring the distance he had put between them.

She would go on loving him as if he were not shutting her out.

Once he had a chance for his temper to cool, surely he would realize love did not prevent him from providing for Aberly.

He'd missed one meeting, but there were bound to be others.

What they felt for one another was a once in a lifetime blessing.

Thinking on it, she had not told him she loved him either, had she? She may have sighed something to the effect in a moment of delirious bliss, but it probably emerged as a sigh not words.

She would correct that error once the proper moment presented.

Chapter Fifteen

Three weeks after River committed his sin against Aberly, and there was no mistaking that was what it had been, he escorted Mr. Levitt though the main room of the suite and bid him goodbye at the door.

The news that Levitt delivered was quite good…and yet it did not absolve him of his indulgence with Lilleth.

The damage had been done.

Ever since, he found himself gazing sidelong at his wife while she went cheerfully about the business of being Viscountess. The trouble was, it was not only his eyes following her, it was his heart, too.

He was having a misery of a time shoving it back in his chest where it belonged.

This was the price he must pay, he feared. Sadder but wiser was the saying.

No sooner had he crossed back to his study than the door opened and the room came alive with chattering female voices.

Lilleth, Clara and Aunt Deborah had their arms loaded with colorful hatboxes.

"River!" Clara set her boxes down then flopped backward onto the couch. "It has been the most exhilarating morning."

"So I see."

Lilleth put her boxes on the floor then crossed the room, went up on her toes. She kissed his cheek.

His wife never failed to smile and speak cheerily to him. To look at her, it was as if nothing earth-shattering had occurred between them.

Surely, she must think him to be the worst of men after he'd loved her and then set her aside.

"It is not the hats, my dear boy, although they are a delight, each and every one of them." Aunt Deborah lifted the lid on one of her boxes then displayed the frilly green bonnet. "We have been invited to Mrs. Staunton's masquerade ball."

"The best people will be there," Clara added. "Invitations are highly sought after."

It might be a problem… "When is it happening?"

"One month from tomorrow. Doesn't a masquerade ball sound thrilling?" Clearly it did to his wife.

He nodded, relieved that he would not need to disappoint in this, at least. "It does, indeed. I look forward to it. And I have other news that we can look forward to."

"Surely not better than dressing up however our fantasies lead." Aunt Deborah waggled her brows. Where did her fantasy lead, he wondered, smiling in spite of himself.

Smiles had been rare for him over the past few weeks but seeing the ladies of the family in such high anticipation was infectious.

Certainly his news would make them even happier.

"I have arranged for passage home. We will sail a few days after the ball."

Everyone seemed delighted except for Lilleth. A look passed behind her smile which he could only guess was uneasiness.

"A word with you, my dear?" He nodded toward the study making sure to maintain his smile. The last thing he wished was for her to be anxious about going to her new home.

My dear, he'd called her. As before she wondered if he meant it or not. But he was giving her a rare smile, so maybe he did.

Hopefully his attitude toward her was beginning to thaw.

"I have some news to share," he said.

"Good news, I hope." He had not invited her to sit so she simply walked about the study looking at this and that item, trying to appear at ease. Which she absolutely was not.

This was the first time they had been alone together since…"the night."

"Exceptional news. The business associate whose meeting I missed when—" River seemed to have lost his words all at once.

"I remember when." As if she could ever forget a second of it.

"Yes…well, he has agreed to reschedule. We will be traveling to London on the same ship and will conduct our business at sea. I thought you would be glad to know."

"That is wonderful news. I did tell you it would all work out for the best."

"At the time I was not best inclined to hear it. But you were right. I will not fail you this time."

"If you think you did last time." Surely she was not blushing after everything…but her cheeks did feel hot. "I promise, River, you did not. I hope through all this you understand that there is more to life than financial success."

"For some men, but not for me."

Viscount Stubborn was what he should be titled. It

wrenched her heart to be reaching out and trying to bring him back to the marriage and all the while feel him slipping away.

"Especially you." She spun about then walked toward the door.

But then she stopped, curled her fingers into fists to gather courage. She turned slowly about, her whispering skirt the only sound in the room.

"I love you, River Halston."

She saw an argument beginning in his eyes so she went out, closing the door behind her.

He needed a moment for the words to sink in, was all. It could not be long before he said them back to her.

Evidently it could be a long time, she thought.

Three weeks had passed and all anyone talked about were costumes for Mrs. Staunton's ball.

Breakfast this morning was no different. Over eggs, muffins, bacon and hot chocolate Aunt Deborah made her final decision.

"I will be a masked garden fairy. My costume will be such delicious fun."

Breakfast was also delicious. The hot chocolate smelled especially nice. Life was more pleasant with the sweet dark drink to begin the day.

She lifted the china cup, and then something happened. She could not press the cup to her lips. Now, that was odd. She set it back on the saucer then ate a piece of bacon instead.

"Mama is going to be a princess," Elizabeth announced. "Aren't you, Mama?"

"She is! With a crown," Violet added.

"Made of diamonds." Victoria's eyes glittered, probably

imagining how she would dance about with her mother's tiara on her own head.

Lilleth picked up the cup again. Her throat closed so she set it back down.

This inability to swallow a drink she loved was beyond puzzling. She hadn't felt anything like it before.

"I will be a shepherdess," Lilleth announced after taking a bite of eggs, which were seasoned to perfection and very delicious. "If your uncle will agree to be my sheep."

"He must agree! It makes a story." Elizabeth clapped her hands. "Mama lives in the castle while Auntie and Uncle live in her pasture."

"And while Auntie Deborah flits about wherever she wishes to," Victoria said. "Auntie Lilleth, if you do not wish to drink your chocolate, may I do it for you?"

Lilleth slid the cup toward her niece. There was nothing wrong with the drink. It smelled as rich and delicious as ever…only she could not drink it.

It was such a mystery…

Until the next morning when she stood at her washbasin losing the breakfast she had yet to eat.

She had noticed her monthly bleeding was late, but surely…

Cleaning the basin, she filled it with water then splashed her face.

Well then…well…there had been another sign her figure was changing. She had never been this full-chested before.

In the end it was remembering the odd moment with the hot chocolate that convinced her.

She glanced down at her flat stomach and touched it.

"Are you there?" she whispered.

It seemed impossible. Such a wonder could not be taking place within her.

And yet it could be. Growing up on a farm, she understood how the miracle began, so yes, it could well have happened.

She would simply have to wait and see what the next days brought.

"If you are there," she whispered, "I love you."

As it turned out, River was not a going to be sheep, but a goat. The costume had been delivered and there was no time to obtain a new one.

With all that needed to be done with scheduling the delivery of their possessions to the boat, he'd spared little thought for the masquerade ball.

His brain was dizzy planning for the transfer of horses, the carriage and the employees he'd brought with him. He shook his head at the trunks stacked in the main room. The number had surely doubled with all the shopping the ladies had been doing.

To add to all he was bringing home, there was now a rambunctious puppy.

And more…much more, he was bringing home a wife. A lovely, smart and funny lady who said she loved him.

Of all that he was taking back, love was what he had not expected. Not what he wanted. It was the heaviest of all the effects he was shipping to England.

It was not as if he could leave emotion behind at the hotel.

The rub was, he would not change how he felt about his wife even if he was able to.

At least that was his thinking in the moment while soaking up the smile she was giving him.

Other times, when he was focused on business, he

thought he might be able to resist the temptation she presented.

Funny, but there was something different about her smile this morning.

She was holding up the goat costume, seeking his approval…but that smile held a secret of some sort.

Mischief maybe? Did she imagine seducing him while he wore it? If she did mean to seduce him…and that glint in her smile indicated she might, it was not going to happen. Curse his fickle mind. He was the one to have imagined the seduction, Lilleth was merely showing him a costume.

All of a sudden, Lilleth's smile sagged. She dropped the costume on the couch.

"If you will excuse me." She dashed for her bedroom.

Moments later she came out looking slightly pale but with her smile returned.

"You must try this on to see if it fits." She wagged the empty goat suit at him. "The ball is tomorrow night."

"And the ship leaves in four days," he pointed out. "Have you heard from your mother? Will she be here to see us off?"

"She and John, both."

Lilleth opened a trunk then sifted through the contents.

"What are you looking for?"

"Feet. The girls were playing with them earlier and I think they ended up—Ah! Here they are." She lifted up a pair of slippers neatly designed as hooves. "You can hardly be a proper goat without cloven feet."

"I'd rather have been something more dashing than a bleating goat."

"Oh, River, you must remember to bleat." Apparently she found more humor in the prospect than he did for she began to laugh. "In your daily life you are a dashing viscount so it only makes sense for your costume to be a humble one. Besides, we shall have great fun playing goat and shepherdess."

She handed him the hooves.

"I refuse to bleat."

"Think of it—I will sway about in my sweet little dress holding my pretty staff and you will follow me loyally about…baaing."

The image in his mind made him laugh before he could prevent it.

"Very well, you are right—we will have a good time."

How could it hurt to share an amusing evening with his wife? It was not as if he could succumb to seducing her behind a pot, nor did he have any business scheduled until they were aboard ship.

Tomorrow night he would enjoy the company of his lovely shepherdess. They would laugh and dance. He would demonstrate his affection for her, stopping only short of admitting his love.

That was a secret he must keep to himself, although in the moment he could not figure out why.

It would come to him later, he was certain.

Lilleth had expected the masquerade to be deliciously fun and it was.

Grooms and princesses daringly flirted with one another while a garden fairy flitted about tapping them on the head with her wand in false censure.

Aunt Deborah even swatted River, the goat, on his tail for appearing as if he would kiss his shepherdess.

Which he did not do.

Oh, he whispered in her ear that she was the most beautiful goat herder in attendance. Of course she was the only one, but still, the words were welcome. It could only be a matter of moments before he lured her to a secluded corner to confess his love.

He was acting like a man who was smitten. Even while dancing with other ladies, which he was required to do, he glanced her way with an expression which surely conveyed that he loved her.

Tonight there was a spark between them which she had not felt since the night of the storm. She had no idea what had changed within River. But how grateful she was to have back the man who had given himself to her that night.

There were times when a person's very soul felt warm and this was one of them.

Tonight she would tell him of the baby on the way. It could only add to the wonder of the evening and make it a moment they would remember with great joy.

As soon as she could get him to a nice secluded corner… or onto a dim path in the garden…but probably not the garden since it was drizzling.

Better, while they were dancing and the romance of the music carried them away…

Maybe not that either since sharing the joy of where their love had led might cause her to trip over the dance steps.

Soon, though…she would know when the moment was right.

When the music ended River bid goodbye to the siren he had been dancing with then cut his way through the crowd, coming her way.

Such a glad expression warmed his gaze that it made her toes dance in her shepherdess boots.

He slipped his arm about her waist, kissed her cheek in a spot that grazed the corner of her mouth.

"River, may we speak…in private?" The happy news she

was about to reveal was singing through her. The melody which the orchestra had just begun was not half as lovely.

River caught her hand; he spun her about. Her skirt made a merry twirl.

"First let's dance."

This was their third dance and he held her closer this time. She felt the pulse in his fingers thrumming on her palm. His eyes gazed down at her with the same affection she'd seen when they were tethered together by a wet rope.

"There is something I want to tell you," she said.

"Wait, let me guess." He grinned down at her. Surely he did not suspect they had been blessed with a child. "It's 'I told you so.' You were correct, being a goat is great fun… baaaaa."

The rush of his soft bleat whispered across her ear.

"Such great fun, but that is not it…"

His gaze slid away, but he continued to smile.

Lilleth looked at what had caught his attention.

An angel, complete with white feathered wings stood at the far side of the ballroom.

Alicia was as stunning as the last time Lilleth had seen her. River claimed he'd not been in love with her, but it seemed that every other man here was.

There was not a male in her vicinity whose head did not swivel while following her progress toward the refreshment room.

She watched the angel turn her heavenly gaze toward River as if sensing he was nearby. Alicia smiled, he nodded back.

"May we speak now?" she asked again, tugging on his sleeve to regain his attention.

"Of course, my dear." He kissed her forehead. "But perhaps after another dance? I will not get the chance to spin my beautiful shepherdess about a ballroom again until after we arrive in London."

"I did not realize I married a flirt."

"You did not. There is not a princess, fairy or siren as appealing as you are."

Hearing him say so was reassuring since she was feeling inelegant in comparison to the angel.

Within seconds she forgot about insecurities. Being held in River's arms, seeing the smile in his eyes…she knew the truth. He did love her even if he could not find the words.

No doubt once she told him about the baby, he would utter them.

Besides, hearts connected by wedding vows and love was what mattered most. Hearing the words would simply confirm what she already knew to be true.

When the dance ended he asked if she was hungry. She was not. In moments she would tell him why.

"Lord Aberly!" Their host hurried toward them waving his hand. "A moment of your time, if you please… I hope you do not mind if I take your husband away for a few moments, Lady Aberly. His opinion is needed on a matter of some interest."

"I do not mind, Mr. Staunton," she replied, managing a smile even though she did mind, very much.

It was proving a difficult thing to give River the most momentous news of his life.

Perhaps she ought to go to the refreshment room and see if she could manage a cracker or two.

The mingled scents coming from the room made her stomach revolt. She sat down on a chair a few feet from the doorway to wait for River to finish his conversation.

From where she sat she could see him on the other side of the room. It must have been a joke since they all began to laugh. She watched River scan the ballroom, probably looking for his “beautiful shepherdess.” Just recalling the expression in his eyes when he’d said so made her warm all over.

His smile was so joyful she thought it likely he was about to tell her he loved her.

But wait! All of a sudden he was bowing over Alicia’s hand, escorting her to the ballroom floor.

His smile had not been for her at all.

The green feeling settling in the pit of her belly must have to do with the baby since there was no reason for her to be jealous. Alicia had never really held River’s heart.

And she would not be uneasy if her husband did not have a particular light in his eye…the very one that had made Lilleth feel cherished all evening.

Three women walking past paused near her chair, partially blocking her view, which, she decided was a good thing. There was no need to borrow trouble where there was none.

“Well, it is as I told you,” a lady dressed as a striped cat declared, her accent announcing her as British.

“You were there in London when it happened?” her companion asked.

“Oh, yes, you can accept what I say as the very truth. I tell you, looking at the pair of them now—it was a great tragedy what happened.”

This was interesting. Lilleth nearly forgot her queasiness.

“Poor Lord Aberly. My heart just breaks for him.”

What was that? Why would her heart break for River?

He had never mentioned a tragedy, nor had Clara or Deborah.

Lilleth's face grew hot and her hands cold. What was this about?

"I cannot imagine how awful it must have been for him to be forced to break off their engagement in order to marry that rich American," the third woman muttered while shaking her head. "Just look at them dancing…the tender way they hold one another. It all but breaks your heart. Anyone can see they are still in love."

But…no! According to her husband, they never had been.

Lilleth peered around the cat's skirt looking for proof that it was not true. She was certain that her husband was in love with her.

And yet he was looking tenderly at the angel. She was looking tenderly at him. Some unspoken message seemed to pass between them.

River laughed. He whispered something in Alicia's ear then twirled her about. Tender emotion, which the whole room must notice, swirled between them.

"But of course they are…or at least Lord Aberly is. All of London witnessed how completely crushed he was when Alicia married so quickly after the split."

"Do you suppose her child is the Viscount's and not her husband's?"

Where was her breath? Her heartbeat? Both stopped. It was as if she'd been knocked flat on the floor.

"I do pity Lady Aberly, though." This voice came to her as though through a fog. Perhaps this was a nightmare from which she would awaken. "She is such a kind and witty lady."

How could she have been so mistaken in her husband's affections toward her? Had she wanted a loving marriage so badly that she had tried to force it? She must have imagined a bond that did not exist.

Nor would it.

All along her efforts to win River over had been useless. Her husband was in love with another woman and always had been.

If there was any way to deny it, she would…but she saw what she saw…and so did others.

What she would not do was give in to the weeping fit swelling in her chest because there was something she was beyond kind, witty and unloved.

She was pretty sure she was going to be a mother. For her child's sake she would rise from this nightmare. No one knew how a mother's distress might harm an unborn child.

Lilleth took a long breath, wrapped the mantle of Viscountess about herself then rose from the bench.

"Pity me?" she asked, taking some satisfaction in the dismay on the women's faces. "Whyever would you?"

"We beg your pardon, Lady Aberly," the cat gasped. "We were unaware that you were sitting behind us."

"Let it be a lesson to you, then. Gossip has consequences." How was Lilleth even standing? Speaking as if they had merely insulted the color of her gown? "Go along now, ladies, and mind your manners."

While Lilleth attempted to gather up the broken pieces of her life, which were jagged and too slippery to grasp, her husband danced with his one true love.

What she ought to do was look away, but she could not make herself do it, even though what she saw made the knife that had been plunged in her heart twist viciously.

There was nothing she wanted more than to call for the carriage and to go home. Almost nothing more. It was unlikely that her chastisement had shut the gossips' mouths.

If she left the party it would only fuel their tittle-tattle about poor brokenhearted Lady Aberly.

Well she was not brokenhearted. She was utterly crushed.

She remained erect and dry-eyed because there was more to be considered than her emotions. She would never have her innocent child learn how its mother had crumpled at a masquerade ball, too distraught to do anything but sob into her beribboned apron.

Lifting her chin and with it her heart, she crossed the ballroom. She greeted Mrs. Johnston with a gracious smile for all to see and after that she danced with her husband.

Somehow she managed to maintain a smile although it did not come from her heart.

Looking into River's eyes while he twirled her about, she felt a dashed fool. How could she have thought him close to admitting he loved her.

Nothing could be further from the truth, she now understood.

At any time he might have told her about how he'd loved this woman he'd been forced to break off his engagement with. But no, he could not, could he? Not without risk of Lilleth changing her mind and him losing the wealth she brought to the marriage.

River Halston was a man who was willing to give up everything, and clearly anyone, in order to advance the viscountcy.

One more thing became clear to her. What to her had been precious hours of intimacy that stormy night had not been to him.

There had been a purpose to it and it was not loving her.

But then, he had not claimed to, had he?

How naive of her to misunderstand every tender touch, every kiss and sigh.

It had all been to one intent, to beget an heir.

"Are you well, my dear?" River asked, jolting her attention back to the dance.

She must not scowl at the false endearment.

But, really? His dear? She was no longer that…as if she had ever been!

No wonder he had looked so uncomfortable when she admitted her love.

Loving one woman and having another…his wife…profess her deepest affection? It must have been awkward for him…extremely so.

Not that she pitied him. Any suffering he went through was caused by his own lordly, falsehearted self.

For appearances sake, she smiled. Outward impressions must be maintained for the good of the title. Aberly meant everything to the Viscount, if no longer to the Viscountess.

She would act her part for the rest of the masquerade and no longer than that.

One thing she had determined over the course of the nightmarish evening was that her child would not be shackled to high society like its father had been.

The ship was leaving for Southampton the day after tomorrow.

Lilleth Halston and child would not be on it.

Chapter Sixteen

The morning after the masquerade ball, River sat at his desk putting together gratuities for the American staff who had served them so loyally during their long stay.

Going about the task, he wondered what had come over Lilleth last night.

One moment she had been playful, the next somber. She had continued to smile, but it was an empty gesture. It was as if she had changed her disguise. From flirtatious shepherdess to woebegone goatherd.

And she had made the transition so skillfully that he was the only one who would have noticed.

Perhaps though, the cause had been no more than a headache that she did not wish to burden anyone with.

Lilleth was not one to add burden, but ease it. She was a rare person who spread goodwill to anyone she met… highborn or low.

His bride was an ideal viscountess through and through.

River felt cheery. In fact, he had not experienced this lightness of heart in a very long time.

It might be due to the fact that he was taking his family home, at long last. While his trip to New York had been successful in every way it could be, he was anxious to board the ship for home.

Once he had everyone and everything settled aboard, he could turn his attention to his business meeting.

He was eager to secure the family's financial stability. Given that this contract would keep the estate secure for years to come perhaps he could stop fearing that loving his wife was a risk to the family's well-being.

No wonder he was in such a happy frame of mind.

Of course, his cheeriness this morning might have also been to do with last night.

He'd had no idea that dressing up as a goat could be so amusing. The reason it had been was because of Lilleth. A comely shepherdess could woo a man like no one else.

First thing when he saw her this morning, he would give her a rousing kiss. It was what he'd wanted to do upon arriving back at the hotel last night, but Lilleth had yawned and gone to her bedroom before a proper good-night could be expressed.

It had been a disappointment since he'd hoped she would come to his chamber and not go to her own.

Also, something important had happened last night. He'd danced with Alicia…laughed with her, spoke with her of her happy marriage and her coming child.

The encounter had been amicable. The bitterness and the guilt he'd felt in regard to her no longer crippled his heart.

For so long he'd believed he would never love another… but last night had proved once and for all how wrong he had been.

In a very real sense, he'd been set free of the wounds of the past.

All along Lilleth had been reaching out for him. Fool that he was, he'd kept her at a distance, choosing rather to wallow in his wounds.

River looked up from the money he'd been staring at to watch dust motes floating in a beam of sunlight.

There was a still a shadow darkening his lighter, freer self.

He'd forgotten about it for a time but now it crept back, dimming his joy.

Only seconds ago, he been ready to declare his love to Lilleth. Just as soon as she came out of her chamber, his plan had been to kiss her and tell her.

Considering the matter, he decided he would need to wait a little bit longer to open his heart. There was his shipboard meeting to be considered. He had been proven correct in that he could not entertain business and pleasure at the same time.

Once the business was successfully completed, he would be the husband Lilleth deserved…the one he wanted very much to be.

River put money in an envelope to give Mr. Gordon, the butler, all the while grinning at dust motes swirling in a beam of sunshine.

Life was good.

But where was Lilleth?

Normally she was an early riser. He hoped her subdued humor last night had not been an indication that she was falling ill.

A few moments later, Lilleth's maid walked past his open study door.

"Millie, is your mistress ill, do you know?"

"Why, I do not think so, sir. Lady Lilleth went out and about her day rather early this morning."

Not ill then, only busy. The same as they all were. Getting ready for the trip across the ocean was a large undertaking. One that he was glad was nearly complete.

An hour later Clara and Aunt Deborah came in the front door, their arms laden with last-moment purchases. It was a wonder there was anything left in the New York shops.

"Isn't Lilleth with you?"

Matching frowns met his gaze.

"I suppose not, then…but do you know where she is?"

"We do not." Aunt Deborah's words sounded stern. The lady never sounded stern.

Before he could puzzle further on her odd behavior, the maid bustled out of Lilleth's bedroom.

"Oh, sir! I've found a note from Lady Aberly addressed to you."

She handed it to him and then went on her way, humming.

"I imagine you should read it," Deborah stated, her frown descending to a glare.

"I do not know what could be so—"

"I feared this might happen," Aunt Deborah said with a sniff.

Unfolding the paper, he read aloud, "'I have gone home. My money is yours, my person is not.'"

What the blazes? Open-mouthed, he stared back and forth from one frowning face to the other.

"You know something which I clearly do not."

Lilleth had gone home and not for a visit!

She'd left him?

What sense did that make after the wonderful evening they'd shared last night?

"River Halston." Clara curled her hands into fists at her waist. "Were you oblivious to what people were saying last night?"

"Apparently, I was." He'd been too caught up in having

a delightful time with his wife to be aware of anything but that. "Gossip was not first on my mind."

"Well, it was about you so it ought to have been. Clearly it was on our Lilleth's mind." Clara narrowed her eyes at him. "I hold you accountable for her going away."

"Yes, dear, as do I," said Aunt Deborah.

"Tell me what you heard." How horrid could it have been?

"Why…" Aunt Deborah said, her eyes gone round. "That you are still in love with Alicia. The pity in the room for our dear girl was palpable."

"In love with Alicia! It is not true."

"Since when is it not?" Clara exclaimed. "You have been mooning about over her ever since you broke off the engagement."

He had yet to tell his wife he was in love with her so it was probably all wrong to tell someone else first but… "Since I fell in love with my wife."

"I see… When did you tell our Lilleth that?" Clara was not asking a question, she was making an accusation.

"I haven't, yet."

"Oh my… I rather think that if you had she would not have gone home, River, dear."

"There was bound to be gossip." Clara flipped an accusing finger at his coat sleeve. "You ought to have been truthful about your feelings for Alicia. At least then our Lilleth would have been forewarned about what she saw last night."

River sat down hard on the couch. "What is it you think she saw?"

"What everyone else did." Clara sat down beside him, took his hand and squeezed. "She saw you and Alicia dancing in one another's arms, laughing and smiling as if nothing had changed even though you had both wed others. You do understand that there were people present last night who recall the breakup and were only too happy to talk about how, from the way you were gazing at each other, you are still in love."

"Deeply in love," Aunt Deborah added.

"That is absurd. I am married to Lilleth and Alicia is married to Hugh!"

"Which only advances the rumor that her child is not Hugh's, but yours."

"What? No! The timing for that does not even ring true."

"Oh, my naive boy." Clara shook her head. "Gossip does not care."

"It seems that my wife does care."

"As she would. You can count on the fact that yapping mouths made certain she heard everything. You, dear brother, must figure out what is to be done about it."

"I am innocent," he protested.

"To a degree, my dear," Aunt Deborah's tone was not all that commiserative.

Clara let go of his hand then stood up. "Come, Aunt, let's find the girls and take them to the park. River will need time to find his way out of this mess so that we may have our Lilleth back."

"Oh dear, there is not much chance of that, is there? The moments are ticking by."

And off they went leaving him with a problem with no solution.

With a choice which he could not make.

It came down to going after his wife and missing the ship and his appointment, or setting sail and leaving his wife behind, perhaps forever.

There was no way the businessman he was going to meet would reschedule, not after River failed to appear for second time. Such irresponsible behavior would not be tolerated.

Word of it would spread.

Curse it though, if he did not go after Lilleth, she would assume he was in love with Alicia and did not mind leaving her behind.

River buried his face in his hands.

Love or obligation…

No man should be forced to make such a decision.

Finally home, Lilleth dashed up the stairway calling for her mother.

At the first sight of Mama coming out of her bedroom holding a gown she was probably packing for her trip to New York, Lilleth started to cry.

She had been strong up until now, doing what she must to get home, but here was Mama.

There was no more need for a brave front.

Her mother dropped the dress then opened her arms.

Lilleth rushed into them the same as she had done countless times since she was a baby. Mama patted her back, crooning that everything would be all right.

Although her mother did not know what was wrong, Lilleth needed to hear those words…to feel the security of loving arms rocking her.

"Come now, sweetheart." Mama stepped over the dress on the floor then led her down the stairs. "We will go to the kitchen and have tea. You may tell me all about why you are here and not preparing to go with your husband to England."

Between sniffles and sips of tea she told her about how River cared for nothing but making money and how he only wanted an heir.

Once the teacup was drained for the third time and her tears dried to salty streaks, Lilleth said, "And so I have come home."

"Of course you have, darling. And where else should you come to? But I think you are wrong about your husband not loving you. I have seen the way he looks at you. He loves you very much."

"If he does he is keeping it a great secret from me."

"As you are keeping one from him?" Mama lifted a brow, smiled softly.

Surely she could not know? But she was Mama and must have an intuition of some sort.

Lilleth nodded. "I did not come home alone. But how could you tell?"

"A mother has a sense of her child. Besides that, your gown never fit you quite that way before." She nodded at Lilleth's bosom. "You will need to tell your husband."

"I suppose it is your mother's sense which tells you I have not?"

"No, dear, it is common sense. If he knew he would never have let you get away."

"I mean to tell him…but I do not mean to live in a foreign country with a man who does not want me."

For some reason that made her mother give a small laugh. "Of course he wants you."

"Ha! What he wants is money and he is willing to put it before anything else. Did you know that he was in love with a woman…was even engaged to her and then broke it off in order to marry me? And he still loves her!"

"Mrs. Johnston, you mean? Yes, dear, I did know that. I would hardly let you wed a man without knowing all about him."

"Apparently everyone knew but me, then."

"Don't worry, Lilleth. This will all work itself out. It is not unusual for marriages to hit a bit of a bump. Love usually wins out in the end. You will see."

"I would say one's husband loving someone else is more than a bit of a bump. Love can hardly win when it does not exist. Besides, he will not put whatever feelings he might have for me above his particularly important meeting he has scheduled while he is at sea."

"We shall see." Mama slid a muffin toward her. Lilleth slid it back.

"The ship leaves for England at dawn tomorrow and Lord Aberly will be on it."

Mama stood up, came around the kitchen table and wrapped her in a tight hug.

"Whatever happens, I am so pleased to be a grandmama."

"And I am pleased to be someone's mama."

A small sweet someone who was not going to a boy burdened with becoming a viscount. Nor would her baby girl live with the knowledge of being an accidental consequence of attempting to get an heir.

This little one would be valued for the person he or she was, and not for what part they played in River's world.

Apple Valley Acres was where her child would be born and raised.

Late the next afternoon Lilleth rode a sweet mare to the cemetery. She relished the breeze fluttering through her hair, the scent of the horse beneath her and acres of grass turning brown under warm autumn sunshine.

Peering into the distance, she saw someone painting the fence. His red hair glinted in a beam of sunlight.

"Homer!"

What a great surprise! She dismounted then tied her horse to a fence post.

"Howdy, Lills! I heard you'd come home." He stood. White paint dripped from the brush and down his wrist.

She had to look away or weep. Her heart saw something other than what her eyes did. Not Homer painting a fence but River, his gaze all mischief and passion…a smear of paint on his cheek from kissing her.

"I'm right happy to see you." Homer set the brush aside and wiped his wrist on the thigh of his pants. White streaks indicated that he had done so before.

"I'm happy to see you, too. Tell me about your ranch. Are things going well?"

"Going well at my ranch and my job here. Sure is a fine fella, that husband of yours. He is one to take care of people."

"That is what is most important to him." She did not tell her friend that, to River, duty was more important than she was.

"Have you heard anything from your family?"

"Adam wrote that they bought a place and hardly remember this one." He grinned. "You wouldn't recognize my ranch anymore, Lills. You can't tell my family was ever there. But for now I'm living in the bunkhouses where the other hands live. Just until I build a proper home on my acres."

All at once he grinned, slapped his thigh with his hat.

"Great Caesar rising! I forgot to tell you the big news."

It must be wonderful. Lilleth could not recall him being so happy before.

"You remember Miss Melinda Grayson? Well, the two of us fell in love and we're to be married next week."

He was young to wed, was what she thought, but what did that matter when he was so head over heels in love.

Melinda was a fortunate young lady.

Unlike Lilleth who was…Never mind. This was not a time for self-pity.

No time was. Life was too full of blessings to indulge in ingratitude.

"I am so happy for you, I could burst." She kissed Homer's cheek, which made him blush. "I should be getting back. Dinner will be waiting."

"I'd be pleased if you'd come to the wedding."

"Just try and keep me away."

Even if the impossible did happen and River came for her, she would not miss Homer and Melinda's joyful day.

Riding back toward the house she took a glance at the long road leading away from the ranch.

In her mind she reviewed every conversation she'd had with River about Alicia. Not once had he given any indication of his the depth of feelings for the woman.

Ha! Her ghost had been between them when he'd spoken his vows!

She would be a fool to believe River was coming for her. The ship was sailing early tomorrow morning. Twelve hours from now.

If her husband meant to come for her, he would have been here by now.

Her intention in returning home had been to get away, not have him chase her down so what did it matter that he had not?

"But I wonder if I made a mistake," she said to the mare who had a sympathetic ear. "Why would River come after a wife who deserted him…especially one he did not love?"

He would not, as the next several hours would prove. The sooner she quit gazing mournfully at the road the better off she would be.

The next afternoon Lilleth decided to walk to the cemetery. This deep into autumn the weather ought to be colder but today sunshine made everything bright and sunny.

Exercise would do her and her baby much good.

She began to sing a light tune, so sweet and melodious that birds would probably join in. A tune so cheerful it might trick her child into believing all was well with its mother.

How far out at sea would the ship be by now? Nine hours if she figured right.

Which of course she had, having felt every moment as a jab in the heart…pump, stab, pump. On and on, it went.

What she needed was to speak with her brothers and Pa. They could give her no answers, but there was always comfort to be found while sitting beside the stones and lovingly tracing the carved names with the tip of her finger.

Eric… Benny…she liked to imagine who they would have become. Fine men, she was certain.

She did not need to imagine Pa. He was always nearby, especially in quiet moments, like this one.

She knelt down, brushed away a yellow leaf from his stone. "Well, Pa, you will know that I married. You will also know that I have come home, and not with my husband. But you do not know…or perhaps you do…but however it works in regard to what you know, you are a grandfather."

All at once a bird chattered merrily in the tree overhead. "I realize it's not really you expressing happiness at the news, but it is nice to imagine."

She also imagined her father tossing a blond-haired child in the air and catching her.

Yawning, Lilleth lay down in a beam of sunshine streaming though the nearly bare branches. She was so sleepy all the time. Mama said it was all a part of carrying a child.

She meant to imagine Papa cradling a little boy in his arms, but her mind changed the image to River holding him.

What a heartrendingly beautiful sight. Her throat clogged at the fantasy.

Tonight she would write her husband a letter and inform him that she had a baby on the way.

She dozed lightly, this time dreaming of her and River together holding their child…singing to it.

Drifting between deep sleep and a doze, the song sounded vivid. River's voice as deep and beautiful as when she'd heard it for real.

"'Beautiful dreamer awake unto me, starlight and dewdrops are waiting for thee, Sounds of the rude world heard in the day, Lull'd by the moonlight have all passed away…'"

There must be a breeze although she did not feel one. But it carried the tune and made it seem as if it came from beside her, close beside her.

She sighed, rolled onto her back and pressed her hand to her middle, wondering if babies had dreams along with their mothers.

As dreams went she had never experienced a better one or one more vivid. She lay quite still, hoping it did not vanish as dreams tended to do.

"'Beautiful dreamer, Queen of my song, List while I woo thee with soft melody, Gone are the cares of life's busy throng…'"

Something brushed her temple. Probably a beetle in the

grass trying to draw her out of her dream and drop her back to sad reality.

She fought to remain in her doze but slowly, reluctantly, she opened her eyes because ugh…a bug.

"'Beautiful dreamer awake unto me…'"

She lifted her fingers, touched the lingering image of her dream lover's face and felt the rasp of his beard.

Rasp? Dreams did not feel raspy!

She jerked upright so quickly she went half woozy.

This was impossible. River should be streaming across the Atlantic Ocean. He should be celebrating his ever-so-important business deal.

"River? Why…but what are you doing here?"

Chapter Seventeen

"I've come for my runaway wife."

"I did not run away. I merely came home. There is a vast difference between the two."

She leaned toward him. His heart leaped thinking she meant to embrace him, but no, she was shifting her weight only to scoot away.

"Did you use your great influence to make the ship wait for your return?"

"Even a viscount cannot do that. No, the ship sailed on time with all our goods. However, not with us."

"Us?"

"Me, Clara, Aunt Deborah and the girls. Oh, and the puppy." He reached for her hand, but she tucked it behind her. "We were at the dock when I told them I was coming for you. They refused to board and insisted on coming with me."

"Truly?" Her gaze softened at that.

"Everyone is up at the house with your mother."

There was so much that needed to be said between them. He hardly knew where to begin. "Why did you run away without a word?"

She stood up, fluffed her skirt. "Again, I did not run

away. I came home. And it was not without a word, there was a note."

"Ah, the note informing me that I could have your funds but not your person."

"Yes, that is the one." With a snap of her skirt she spun about and began to walk in the direction of the house.

Quite clearly he was more relieved to see her than she was to see him. River got up from the grass and followed her.

"I choose you," he called.

"In the note I was not indicating that there was a choice," she stated with a glance over her shoulder.

After a few more steps she turned again, speared him a pointed look. "But I am curious what you mean by saying that."

"I choose you over securing a fortune."

"Ha! You, Lord Aberly, are a man who will always choose money over love."

"Not always." He caught up with her, touched her elbow to keep her from dashing off. "Here I am. The business associate I stood up is on his way to Southampton."

"Ha again! Did you not choose my money over your great, undying love for the woman you were to wed? That proves you will always choose wealth."

Curse him for a fool, had he been honest with her from the start, had he been the husband she deserved from the very moment he recited his vows, he would not be in this mess.

"Lilleth, I choose you… I love you."

Hearing the confession, she did not joyfully embrace him. But she did not yank her arm away, either.

"Everyone at the masquerade believed you to be in love

with your poor jilted fiancée. They felt a great deal of pity for the pair of you…but more for me."

"Only part of what you just said is true. I did jilt her. And yes, I confess, I did have a time of it getting over her. But I did. When you and I wed all that remained of that love was fear of living through such pain again."

"Humph!" She yanked her arm out of his grip. With a dramatic spin she presented her back. "You might have told me that before."

An awful sense of loss came over him. His wife was standing only feet from him and yet a chasm was widening between them.

It seemed that there was a very real chance that she would not allow him back into her life. The pain he'd felt at losing Alicia would be a tickle in comparison to losing Lilleth.

Not willing to give up, he pressed his case. "Despite what others might have believed at the masquerade, I am not in love with her."

She spun back to face him, her fists clenched in her skirt. "I saw the two of you dancing, River! It looked very much like you were. There was love shining out of your eyes."

"There was and I won't deny it. But it was for you. I was telling Mrs. Johnston how happy I was and that I was pleased she was happy, too."

"You were?"

He was ashamed of himself, seeing the relief misting her eyes. His wife should never have been put in a position to doubt his affection.

Grabbing her to him he hugged her tight, his head bent to her ear.

"My love is only for you…always for you." He lifted

her chin, kissed her softly, praying that she would not push him away.

There had been several hours after he discovered that she was gone when he was not sure if he would hold his wife again.

He touched his forehead to hers, closed his eyes. "I will not let you doubt my love for you again."

Although they were still a distance from the house, those inside must have been watching for all of a sudden the front door flew open wide.

His nieces dashed across the yard then stood under the rose arbor. Clara ran behind, lifting her skirt in her hurry to get to them.

His mother-in-law and his aunt watched from the front porch.

No doubt they were wanting to see if they would need to kill him as they had promised to do if he did not bring their Lilleth back to them with a smile on her face.

"Will you come home to London with me…with all of us?"

"We will speak of London later tonight," she told him.

She was not smiling.

The big clock downstairs chimed midnight. The "later tonight" that Lilleth promised her husband had just turned to the wee hours of the morning.

She put on her robe but did not go to the effort to tie the ribbon to hold it closed.

This was going to be a difficult conversation, but putting it off would do no one any good.

Hopefully, River was not asleep. If so she would have to wake him.

The anxiety clutching her nerves could not be healthy for the baby any more than it was for her.

Sick with dread was not how she wished to tell her husband they were expecting a child. However, what he wanted for the baby's future and what she wanted were miles apart.

Only hours ago River had declared his heart. After what she was about to tell him, she feared he would take it back.

"Do not worry, little one," she murmured, stroking her still-flat stomach. "I will protect you. Society's rules will not hurt you. You will be free to live as you wish."

River's bedroom door was across the hallway from hers.

Crossing over felt like walking a mile.

Hesitating, her hand gripping the doorknob, she sent a silent message from her heart to her child's. "No matter how this works out, you are loved."

Would River's door be locked?

Would he be asleep or waiting for her?

Would she be able to express her thoughts or would they get stuck in her throat?

Would she turn the knob or turn back to her bedroom?

Her mind was getting dizzy, then all at once the door opened.

River drew her inside and wrapped her in a hug.

"I was beginning to fear you were not coming."

He tipped her face up, gave her a long, lingering kiss.

She gave herself over to it, but only for a few seconds.

There was a blessing to be revealed…a very precious person whose future needed deciding.

"Come and sit with me by the fireplace," she said and began to walk toward it.

"The bed is on the other side of the room and I mean to lure you to it."

"We need to speak, River." She withdrew her hand then crossed to the chair and sat down.

Apparently undaunted by her serious tone he stood behind her chair where he proceeded to draw her robe off of her shoulders.

How was she to express a logical point when his thumbs traced delightfully warm circles on her arms…then the hollow of her throat.

No words were getting past that.

And the bed did look inviting with the covers turned down and the pillows fluffed. No doubt the sheets were warm, too. Even if they were not, her husband had the skills to heat them.

When River bent to whisper, "I love you," against the ticklish shell of her ear…well, it was all she could do not to grab the lapels of his robe and drag him across the room.

She reminded herself that she had come to his room for a purpose and leaping into his bed was not it.

"I did say I needed to speak with you…about London."

She stood up because she could not have his hands on her for another second. Those large fingers of his expressed love in a way more seductive than words.

"I will not stop telling you I love you until I know you believe it." He stepped around the chair, slipped his arm around her waist, drew her to this heart. "We can speak about going home while under the covers."

"River Halston, once you get me there, I will not be able to form a thought, and you know it."

"That is my intention."

"You will want to know what I have to say…it is not news which can wait any longer."

He angled in for a kiss, clearly not appreciating the enormity of the news. Without layers of stiff clothing between them the sizzle was enough to make her forget what she was about.

Nearly so, anyway.

What she must keep in mind was that while he claimed to love her now, he might not in a few moments. His idea of what made for a family and her idea of it, were not at all the same.

So, she leaned back in order to put breathing distance between her lips and his kiss.

"River…we are having a child."

He continued on kissing her, walked her backward toward the bed…then suddenly stopped, his brain seeming to catch up with his hearing.

He stared at her for a moment and then swooped her up, spun her about while he laughed.

"Do you mean to tell me we may have achieved our heir on the first try?"

"Put me down, River. That is not at all what I mean."

"But you just told me—"

"We are having a child. But no son of mine will be forced to play the role you have had to. I cannot see that it has led to your happiness."

"Can you not?" He didn't set her down on the carpet but snuggled her more securely to himself. "It was my position in Society which led me to you…so yes, I promise you, it did lead to the greatest joy of my life."

He kissed her again before saying, "Our firstborn son must be an heir, Lilleth, there is no way around it."

"Our firstborn son will be a rancher if he wishes. I have made up my mind…put me down."

He took a step closer to the bed. "What is to say he cannot be both? He has both of us in him."

"You would agree to that?" she asked, not all that certain he meant it.

"I agree to doing whatever will make our children happy."

"And how many children would that be? You know I want several."

"Yes, as do I."

"You do not. You told me what you want—an heir and a spare. Which I still say is a heartless sentiment. I hope we have only girls in order to prevent such a thing."

He stared down at her stomach, touched it gently.

"It was heartless. I regret saying it. I was so ignorant then, Lilleth. But now that you've opened my heart to love, I want as many young Halstons as we are lucky enough to have."

"You do?" Relief washed over her—it rolled out of her heart and through her limbs, fingers and toes. "I will want several."

Still, there was more to be discussed. It might put a strain on River's newly changed outlook on family.

"There is one more thing. I wish to raise our children half of the year at Apple Valley Acres and half of the year in England."

This was where he would give her an argument, no doubt. For a man like River his title was all important and there were not titles in America.

"That would be appropriate since this child…and those to come," he said with a grin, "are both American and British. Besides, I like it here. There is plenty of business to be had in New York. But more than that, there is your mother to think of. She should not have to sail an ocean to see her grandchildren."

"Who are you?" she asked. Surely not the man she had left at the Sutter Hotel.

He cupped her cheeks, gave her a look that made her shiver…or melt. She did not know how she could be feeling both at once but she did know this…

"I love you so much, River. I do regret running away."

"So you do admit you did?"

"I do, although I had just cause."

"Sweet wife, if you had not, we might not be standing here now…inching our way to that bed."

"Yet here we are in spite of ourselves."

"Thank the Good Lord for it." His lips touched hers, a delightful blend of a kiss and a smile. "You and I are going to have a beautiful life."

The next she knew she was on the bed and River was taking a long, delicious time proving his point.

It was a beautiful life.

Epilogue

Ten years later, Christmas Eve,
Apple Valley Acres

The children were far too excited that Santa's boots would soon pop into view coming down the chimney to fall asleep.

As the family tradition had developed, Benny, Claire and Eric lay on blankets and pillows watching for the momentous event to occur.

River snuggled three-year-old Miranda to his heart, relieved that she had gotten over her cold in time to enjoy the night's excitement.

New to the Christmas Eve tradition was three-month-old Beatrice. His baby daughter lay in her mother's arms resisting sleep. It was a battle she would soon lose if her drooping eyelids were anything to go by. He'd held his youngest close to his heart often enough to know she would soon be deeply asleep.

"After the day we've had, I imagine they will all be asleep before long," Lilleth said, stroking Beatrice's downy hair.

The morning had begun with a breakfast party for the ranch hands and their families, hosted by Mr. and Mrs. John Dalton. Mama and John had wed seven years before.

John was an excellent property manager. The ranch had thrived under his care. River was grateful to have him as part of the family.

Homer seemed like family, too. Over the years he'd made a success of his ranch. He and his wife were the parents of four boys, all having their father's red hair.

After the party, Lilleth and River had taken their children to deliver gifts to the orphans at Mary Clinger's Home for Children.

Snow had started to fall on the way home so the sleigh ride back to the ranch had been exciting and hopefully tuckered the little ones out.

So far, it did not seem so.

River sat for a moment, watching snowflakes drift past the windows on either side of the fireplace and listening to the children's voices while they chatted excitedly about what Santa would bring.

There had been a time in his life when he did not believe that such contentment was possible for him…

"Shall we wager on who will fall asleep first?" Lilleth asked.

This waiting for Santa in front of the fireplace was tradition for the children. But there was another tradition, which came after this one, having to do with only him and his wife.

"Eric will be first, I predict," he gave his eldest son a wink. "Then Claire and Benny. Miranda will be last… maybe she will stay awake so long she'll hear reindeer on the roof."

"I will hear them, Papa! I will go up the chimney and ride one."

"You can't do that!" Eric sat up and frowned back at his little sister. "You'll get burned in the fire."

"He's so responsible," Lilleth said, leaning sideways to whisper. "Of them all he is most like you. I imagine he will be an excellent viscount one day."

"I promise to make him understand that his happiness comes first."

He gave his wife a kiss. How could he not? She was more beautiful now than she had been when they wed. Ten years had done nothing but make her lovelier.

He was certain that he was the envy of every gentleman in London and New York.

Not only was his viscountess lovely to look at but she was his sunshine on a rainy day.

Charities in both cities thrived because of her generosity.

"Papa, you are squishing me!" Miranda, stuck between her parents' kiss, wriggled down from his lap and took up watch beside her siblings.

Eric clutched her hand, probably worried that she was considering braving the flames to ride a reindeer.

As it turned out, he was the one to fall asleep first.

River carried his eldest upstairs to his bedroom.

"One down," he said, snuggling back on the couch with his wife.

"Don't get too comfortable, here's another." Lilleth handed him up the baby. She sagged sweetly, trustingly in his arms.

"Have I thanked you lately for convincing me that I wanted to be a father?"

"This time last year, was the last time you mentioned it, I believe."

"I will further demonstrate my gratitude once the others have fallen asleep."

Loving one another on this night of nights was the best

of traditions. One which had resulted in both Benny and Beatrice.

Coming back downstairs he found the remaining three of his children still awake, but fading.

"I hope Mr. Rawlins was not terribly upset that you ended your meeting with him before the deal was completed this morning. But you must admit the party was a great deal more fun."

"I did invite him to stay. He may find another investor if he's displeased. But you did send him off with a yuletide cake so I expect we shall see him next week."

"Look, there go Claire and Benny. They blinked out at the same time."

"It looks like you are the last one awake, Miranda," Lilleth said.

"Do I get a prize?"

"I think your papa should get the prize since he is the one who guessed you would be last to fall asleep."

The glance his wife gave him was an indication of what his prize would be.

He took the steps two at a time anxious to get Claire and Benny up the stairs and into bed.

Dashing back downstairs, he grinned finding Miranda splayed across a pillow, soundly asleep with her thumb in her mouth.

"Victory is ours," he announced. "Do not move from that spot."

"At long last," she agreed and then covered a yawn with the back of her hand.

"Whatever you do, do not fall asleep."

"Oh, I will not…someone's existence might depend upon it."

"I love you," he called back over his shoulder while settling Miranda securely in his arms for a quick run up the stairs.

"I love you, too!"

He'd had the thought a thousand times over the years and would have it thousands of times more…

This was a beautiful life, indeed.

* * * * *

If you enjoyed this story, be sure to check out these Historical romances from Carol Arens

The Rancher's Convenient Wife
The Truth Behind the Governess
Marriage Charade with the Heir
The Gentleman's Cinderella Bride

Or let yourself be swept up in her charming The Rivenhall Weddings miniseries

Inherited as the Gentleman's Bride
In Search of a Viscountess
A Family for the Reclusive Baron